A Washington Square Press Publication of
POCKET BOOKS, a division of Simon & Schuster, Inc.
1230 Avenue of the Americas, New York, N.Y. 10020

ISBN: 0-671-66914-1

First Pocket Books printing February 1968

10 9 8 7 6

WASHINGTON SQUARE PRESS and WSP colophon are
registered trademarks of Simon & Schuster, Inc.

Printed in the U.S.A.

THE FOLGER LIBRARY SHAKESPEARE

Designed to make Shakespeare's classic plays available to the general reader, each edition contains a reliable text with modernized spelling and punctuation, scene-by-scene plot summaries, and explanatory notes clarifying obscure and obsolete expressions. An interpretive essay and accounts of Shakespeare's life and theater form an instructive preface to each play.

Louis B. Wright, General Editor, was the Director of the Folger Shakespeare Library from 1948 until his retirement in 1968. He is the author of *Middle-Class Culture in Elizabethan England, Religion and Empire, Shakespeare for Everyman,* and many other books and essays on the history and literature of the Tudor and Stuart periods.

Virginia Lamar, Assistant Editor, served as research assistant to the Director and Executive Secretary of the Folger Shakespeare Library from 1946 until her death in 1968. She is the author of *English Dress in the Age of Shakespeare* and *Travel and Roads in England,* and coeditor of William Strachey's *Historie of Travell into Virginia Britania.*

Preface

This edition of *Pericles* is designed to make available a readable text of a romance that is not entirely of Shakespeare's composition but that exemplifies a popular type of drama in the closing years of Shakespeare's career. In the centuries since Shakespeare, many changes have occurred in the meanings of words, and some clarification of Shakespeare's vocabulary may be helpful. To provide the reader with necessary notes in the most accessible format, we have placed them on the pages facing the text that they explain. We have tried to make them as brief and simple as possible. Preliminary to the text we have also included a brief statement of essential information about Shakespeare and his stage. Readers desiring more detailed information should refer to the books suggested in the references, and if still further information is needed, the bibliographies in those books will provide the necessary clues to the literature of the subject.

The early texts of Shakespeare's plays provide only scattered stage directions and no indications of setting, and it is conventional for modern editors to add these to clarify the action. Such additions, and additions to entrances and exits, as well as many indications of act and scene divisions, are placed in square brackets.

All illustrations are from material in the Folger Library collections.

L. B. W.
V. A. L.

June 1, 1967

A Greek Romance for Shakespeare's Stage

The play of *Pericles, Prince of Tyre*, probably dating
from 1608-09, was acted in a period when tales de-
rived from ancient Greek romances were becoming
popular on the London stage. It immediately pre-
cedes the late romances that are undoubtedly of
Shakespeare's authorship, and scholars have generally agreed that Shakespeare had a hand in its composition but was not responsible for the entire play.
No general agreement, however, exists as to precisely which parts Shakespeare wrote and which
were the work of another. Most opinion leans to the
view that someone else wrote most of Acts I and II
and that Shakespeare was responsible for most of
Acts III-V. Edmond Malone, in the eighteenth century, suggested that some friend of Shakespeare
wrote the play and that Shakespeare helped to
strengthen the dialogue, especially the last act.
"Without accepting the speculation about Shakespeare's friendship," Professor Geoffrey Bullough
comments, "I accept the conclusion (held by many
other critics) that he [Shakespeare] revised someone else's play."

The attempt to parcel out the portions that may be
Shakespeare's and may be another's has occupied the
ingenuity of many scholars, but no conclusive so-
lution is likely to be found. Most modern scholars

think the brothel scenes and the dialogue with the fishermen have a Shakespearean ring.

One difficulty in analyzing the qualities of the play stems from the miserable text that survives. For what reason we do not know, *Pericles* was not printed in the First Folio of 1623, perhaps because Heminges and Condell, who put together the Folio, did not have an accurate text of the play to print. *Pericles* was first brought out in a quarto version in 1609 as *The Late, And much admired Play, Called Pericles, Prince of Tyre.... As it hath been diuers and sundry times acted by his Maiesties Seruants, at the Globe on the Banck-side. By William Shakespeare.* The text was so corrupt that *Pericles* is usually listed among those versions known to Shakespeare bibliographers as "bad quartos." It bears evidence of having been "reported" either from the memory of one or two actors or in shorthand. At any rate, verse is often printed as prose, and verse lines are frequently imperfect. Some lines are so corrupt as to make their interpretation a puzzle. Editors, who perforce must base an edition on this first printing, have to emend and correct passages as best they can.

The play was so popular with the reading public that six quarto versions were called for by 1635. Each succeeding quarto, however, was essentially a reprint of the previous one, with only such corrections as the printers chose to make and with further corruptions. None of these later quartos has any validity greater than the first. The play was not included in the Second Folio, but, when the printers of the Third Folio in 1664 added seven plays which they

Ancient Gower.
From George Wilkins, *Pericles, Prince of Tyre*, edited by J. P. Collier (1857).

chose to attribute to Shakespeare, they included *Pericles* in the second issue of that edition. For all the scholarly ingenuity and skill lavished upon the study of *Pericles*, this play remains one of the most puzzling that Shakespeare had a hand in.

The ultimate source of the play goes back to classical antiquity, to a tale of Apollonius of Tyre, and it survived in a variety of forms through the Middle Ages and Renaissance. Professor Bullough reports that the tale is still repeated orally by Greek shepherds. A contemporary of Chaucer's, John Gower, retold the story in his collection entitled *Confessio Amantis*. It also appears in another medieval collection of tales, the *Gesta Romanorum*. The tale of Apollonius of Tyre was also excerpted and printed separately. Lawrence Twyne printed the story about 1594 as *The Patterne of Painefull Adventures*, and another edition attributed to Lawrence's brother, Thomas, was published in 1607. The play derives from both Gower's *Confessio Amantis* and *The Patterne of Painefull Adventures*.

The name Pericles has nothing to do with the historical Pericles of Athens. The play probably adapted the name Pyrocles from one of the heroes in Sir Philip Sidney's *Arcadia*.

Another parallel to the story of the play is a prose romance by George Wilkins entitled *The Painfull Adventures of Pericles Prince of Tyre. Being the true History of the Play of Pericles, as it was lately presented by the worthy and ancient Poet Iohn Gower* (1608). This publication appeared a year before the printing of the First Quarto. But in the preface Wilkins begs his readers "to receiue this Historie in the same maner as it was vnder the habite of ancient Gower the famous English Poet by the Kings Maiesties Players excellently presented." Some scholars have argued that Wilkins, who was also a dramatist, may have been Shakespeare's collaborator in *Pericles*. Sir Edmund Chambers remarks that "The relation of the novel to the play is obscure." The probability is that Wilkins was capitalizing upon a popular dramatic hit by getting out a prose version.

For, strange as it may seem to a modern reader or playgoer, *Pericles* was a success, as attested by its six printed editions and by contemporary references to stage versions. This was a period when tragicomedy was coming into popularity, when plays with fantastic settings in faraway opera lands attracted attention, when no absurdities concerned with the recovery of lost children and wives long-believed-dead were too great to gain acceptance on the stage. Shakespeare himself in *The Winter's Tale* was shortly to present another of these romances to please a public which had acquired an appetite for this sort of thing. It is not hard to understand that a Shakespearean audience would have found *Pericles* acceptable and made much of it. This romance for centuries had attracted and entertained listeners who heard it read or recited.

Although Shakespeare occasionally uses a Chorus to report events that cannot be presented easily on the stage, as in *Henry V*, *Pericles* is unusual in depending upon a "presenter" in the person of Gower to tell the audience what it needs to know. Through-

out the play Gower appears to explain and to clarify
the action. Although the play has some fine lines here
and there in the later portions, it is not characteristic
of Shakespeare's usual style and technique.

Pericles enjoyed considerable popularity through
the Jacobean period; on the reopening of the theatres after the Puritan Interregnum, it was one of the
plays chosen for revival in 1660, apparently with
some success. Other plays, however, soon crowded
it off the boards. But in 1738 George Lillo undertook
to revise it and brought out a three-act version entitled *Marina*, which, as its title implies, concentrated
action upon the heroine. Lillo's play did not have a
long life. *Pericles* was revived again in the mid-nine-
teenth century and has had occasional revivals from
time to time, usually by academic or experimental
groups. But not since Shakespeare's day has it
been popular in the professional theatre. During the
season of 1967, the Oregon Shakespearean Festival
at Ashland, Oregon, staged *Pericles* successfully.
Their performance, played straight as the drama was
written, once more proved that Shakespeare and his
collaborator or collaborators knew precisely what
were the requirements of the stage. They were writing for playhouse performance, not for later critics.

THE AUTHOR

As early as 1598 Shakespeare was so well known as
a literary and dramatic craftsman that Francis
Meres, in his *Palladis Tamia: Wits Treasury*, referred in flattering terms to him as "mellifluous and

honey-tongued Shakespeare," famous for his *Venus and Adonis*, his *Lucrece*, and "his sugared sonnets," which were circulating "among his private friends." Meres observes further that "as Plautus and Seneca are accounted the best for comedy and tragedy among the Latins, so Shakespeare among the English is the most excellent in both kinds for the stage," and he mentions a dozen plays that had made a name for Shakespeare. He concludes with the remark that "the Muses would speak with Shakespeare's fine filed phrase if they would speak English."

To those acquainted with the history of the Elizabethan and Jacobean periods, it is incredible that anyone should be so naïve or ignorant as to doubt the reality of Shakespeare as the author of the plays that bear his name. Yet so much nonsense has been written about other "candidates" for the plays that it is well to remind readers that no credible evidence that would stand up in a court of law has ever been adduced to prove either that Shakespeare did not write his plays or that anyone else wrote them. All the theories offered for the authorship of Francis Bacon, the Earl of Derby, the Earl of Oxford, the Earl of Hertford, Christopher Marlowe, and a score of other candidates are mere conjectures spun from the active imaginations of persons who confuse hypothesis and conjecture with evidence.

As Meres's statement of 1598 indicates, Shakespeare was already a popular playwright whose name carried weight at the box office. The obvious reputation of Shakespeare as early as 1598 makes the effort to prove him a myth one of the most absurd in the history of human perversity.

The anti-Shakespeareans talk darkly about a plot of vested interests to maintain the authorship of Shakespeare. Nobody has any vested interest in Shakespeare, but every scholar is interested in the truth and in the quality of evidence advanced by special pleaders who set forth hypotheses in place of facts.

The anti-Shakespeareans base their arguments upon a few simple premises, all of them false. These false premises are that Shakespeare was an unlettered yokel without any schooling, that nothing is known about Shakespeare, and that only a noble lord or the equivalent in background could have written the plays. The facts are that more is known about Shakespeare than about most dramatists of his day, that he had a very good education, acquired in the Stratford Grammar School, that the plays show no evidence of profound book learning, and that the knowledge of kings and courts evident in the plays is no greater than any intelligent young man could have picked up at second hand. Most anti-Shakespeareans are naïve and betray an obvious snobbery. The author of their favorite plays, they imply, must have had a college diploma framed and hung on his study wall like the one in their dentist's office, and obviously so great a writer must have had a title or some equally significant evidence of exalted social background. They forget that genius has a way of cropping up in unexpected places and that none of the great creative writers of the world got his inspiration in a college or university course.

William Shakespeare was the son of John Shakespeare of Stratford-upon-Avon, a substantial citizen of that small but busy market town in the center of the rich agricultural county of Warwick. John Shakespeare kept a shop, what we would call a general store; he dealt in wool and other produce and gradually acquired property. As a youth, John Shakespeare had learned the trade of glover and leather worker. There is no contemporary evidence that the elder Shakespeare was a butcher, though the anti-Shakespeareans like to talk about the ignorant "butcher's boy of Stratford." Their only evidence is a statement by gossipy John Aubrey, more than a century after William Shakespeare's birth, that young William followed his father's trade, and when he killed a calf, "he would do it in a high style and make a speech." We would like to believe the story true, but Aubrey is not a very credible witness.

John Shakespeare probably continued to operate a farm at Snitterfield that his father had leased. He married Mary Arden, daughter of his father's landlord, a man of some property. The third of their eight children was William, baptized on April 26, 1564, and probably born three days before. At least, it is conventional to celebrate April 23 as his birthday.

The Stratford records give considerable information about John Shakespeare. We know that he held several municipal offices including those of alderman and mayor. In 1580 he was in some sort of legal difficulty and was fined for neglecting a summons of the Court of Queen's Bench requiring him to appear at Westminster and be bound over to keep the peace.

As a citizen and alderman of Stratford, John Shakespeare was entitled to send his son to the grammar school free. Though the records are lost, there can be no reason to doubt that this is where young William received his education. As any student of the period knows, the grammar schools provided the basic education in Latin learning and literature. The Elizabethan grammar school is not to be confused with modern grammar schools. Many cultivated men of the day received all their formal education in the grammar schools. At the universities in this period a student would have received little training that would have inspired him to be a creative writer. At Stratford young Shakespeare would have acquired a familiarity with Latin and some little knowledge of Greek. He would have read Latin authors and become acquainted with the plays of Plautus and Terence. Undoubtedly, in this period of his life he received that stimulation to read and explore for himself the world of ancient and modern history which he later utilized in his plays. The youngster who does not acquire this type of intellectual curiosity *before* college days rarely develops as a result of a college course the kind of mind Shakespeare demonstrated. His learning in books was anything but profound, but he clearly had the probing curiosity that sent him in search of information, and he had a keenness in the observation of nature and of mankind that finds reflection in his poetry.

There is little documentation for Shakespeare's boyhood. There is little reason why there should be. Nobody knew that he was going to be a dramatist about whom any scrap of information would be prized in the centuries to come. He was merely an active and vigorous youth of Stratford, perhaps assisting his father in his business, and no Boswell bothered to write down facts about him. The most important record that we have is a marriage license issued by the Bishop of Worcester on November 27, 1582, to permit William Shakespeare to marry Anne Hathaway, seven or eight years his senior; furthermore, the Bishop permitted the marriage after reading the banns only once instead of three times, evidence of the desire for haste. The need was explained on May 26, 1583, when the christening of Susanna, daughter of William and Anne Shakespeare, was recorded at Stratford. Two years later, on February 2, 1585, the records show the birth of twins to the Shakespeares, a boy and a girl who were christened Hamnet and Judith.

What William Shakespeare was doing in Stratford during the early years of his married life, or when he went to London, we do not know. It has been conjectured that he tried his hand at schoolteaching, but that is a mere guess. There is a legend that he left Stratford to escape a charge of poaching in the park of Sir Thomas Lucy of Charlecote, but there is no proof of this. There is also a legend that when first he came to London he earned his living by holding horses outside a playhouse and presently was given employment inside, but there is nothing better than eighteenth-century hearsay for this. How Shakespeare broke into the London theatres as a dramatist and actor we do not know. But lack of information is not surprising, for Elizabethans did not write their autobiographies, and we know even less about the lives of many writers and some men of affairs than we know about Shakespeare. By 1592 he was so well established and popular that he incurred the envy of the dramatist and pamphleteer Robert Greene, who referred to him as an "upstart crow . . . in his own conceit the only Shake-scene in a country." From this time onward, contemporary allusions and references in legal documents enable the scholar to chart Shakespeare's career with greater accuracy than is possible with most other Elizabethan dramatists.

By 1594 Shakespeare was a member of the company of actors known as the Lord Chamberlain's Men. After the accession of James I, in 1603, the company would have the sovereign for their patron and would be known as the King's Men. During the period of its greatest prosperity, this company would have as its principal theatres the Globe and the Blackfriars. Shakespeare was both an actor and a shareholder in the company. Tradition has assigned him such acting roles as Adam in *As You Like It* and the Ghost in *Hamlet*, a modest place on the stage that suggests that he may have had other duties in the management of the company. Such conclusions, however, are based on surmise.

What we do know is that his plays were popular and that he was highly successful in his vocation. His first play may have been *The Comedy of Errors*, acted perhaps in 1591. Certainly this was one of his earliest plays. The three parts of *Henry VI* were acted sometime between 1590 and 1592. Critics are not in agreement about precisely how much Shakespeare wrote of these three plays. *Richard III* probably dates from 1593. With this play Shakespeare captured the imagination of Elizabethan audiences, then enormously interested in historical plays. With *Richard III* Shakespeare also gave an interpretation pleasing to the Tudors of the rise to power of the grandfather of Queen Elizabeth. From this time onward, Shakespeare's plays followed on the stage in rapid succession: *Titus Andronicus, The Taming of the Shrew, The Two Gentlemen of Verona, Love's Labor's Lost, Romeo and Juliet, Richard II, A Midsummer Night's Dream, King John, The Merchant of Venice, Henry IV (Parts 1 and 2), Much Ado about Nothing, Henry V, Julius Caesar, As You Like It, Twelfth Night, Hamlet, The Merry Wives of Windsor, All's Well That Ends Well, Measure for Measure, Othello, King Lear*, and nine others that followed before Shakespeare retired completely, about 1613.

In the course of his career in London, he made enough money to enable him to retire to Stratford with a competence. His purchase on May 4, 1597, of New Place, then the second-largest dwelling in Stratford, "a pretty house of brick and timber," with a handsome garden, indicates his increasing prosperity. There his wife and children lived while he busied himself in the London theatres. The summer before he acquired New Place, his life was darkened by the death of his only son, Hamnet, a child of eleven. In May, 1602, Shakespeare purchased one hundred and seven acres of fertile farmland near Stratford and a few months later bought a cottage and garden across the alley from New Place. About 1611, he seems to have returned permanently to Stratford, for the next year a legal document refers to him as "William Shakespeare of Stratford-upon-Avon . . . gentleman." To achieve the desired appellation of gentleman, William Shakespeare had seen to it that the College of Heralds in 1596 granted his father a coat of arms. In one step he thus became a second-generation gentleman.

Shakespeare's daughter Susanna made a good match in 1607 with Dr. John Hall, a prominent and prosperous Stratford physician. His second daughter, Judith, did not marry until she was thirty-one years old, and then, under somewhat scandalous circumstances, she married Thomas Quiney, a Stratford vintner. On March 25, 1616, Shakespeare made his will, bequeathing his landed property to Susanna, £300 to Judith, certain sums to other relatives, and his second-best bed to his wife, Anne. Much has been made of the second-best bed, but the legacy probably indicates only that Anne liked that particular bed. Shakespeare, following the practice of the time, may have already arranged with Susanna for his wife's care. Finally, on April 23, 1616, the anniversary of his birth, William Shakespeare died, and he was buried on April 25 within the chancel of Trinity Church, as befitted an honored citizen. On August 6, 1623, a few months before the publication of the collected edition of Shakespeare's plays, Anne Shakespeare joined her husband in death.

THE PUBLICATION OF HIS PLAYS

During his lifetime Shakespeare made no effort to publish any of his plays, though eighteen appeared in print in single-play editions known as quartos. Some of these are corrupt versions known as "bad quartos." No quarto, so far as is known, had the author's approval. Plays were not considered "literature" any more than most radio and television scripts today are considered literature. Dramatists sold their plays outright to the theatrical companies and it was usually considered in the company's interest to keep plays from getting into print. To achieve a reputation as a man of letters, Shakespeare wrote his *Sonnets* and his narrative poems, *Venus and Adonis* and *The Rape of Lucrece*, but he probably never dreamed that his plays would establish his reputation as a literary genius. Only Ben Jonson, a man known for his colossal conceit, had the crust to call his plays *Works*, as he did when he published an edition in 1616. But men laughed at Ben Jonson.

After Shakespeare's death, two of his old colleagues in the King's Men, John Heminges and Henry Condell, decided that it would be a good thing to print, in more accurate versions than were then available, the plays already published and eighteen additional plays not previously published in quarto. In 1623 appeared *Mr. William Shakespeares Comedies, Histories, & Tragedies. Published according to the True Originall Copies. London. Printed by Isaac Iaggard and Ed. Blount.* This was the famous First Folio, a work that had the authority of Shakespeare's associates. The only play commonly attributed to Shakespeare that was omitted in the First Folio was *Pericles*. In their preface, "To the great Variety of Readers," Heminges and Condell state that whereas "you were abused with diverse stolen and surreptitious copies, maimed and deformed by the frauds and stealths of injurious impostors that exposed them, even those are now offered to your view cured and perfect of their limbs; and all the rest, absolute in their numbers, as he conceived them." What they used for printer's copy is one of the vexed problems of scholarship, and skilled bibliographers have devoted years of study to the question of the relation of the "copy" for the First Folio to Shakespeare's manuscripts. In some cases it is clear that the editors corrected printed quarto versions of the plays, probably by comparison with playhouse scripts. Whether these scripts were in Shakespeare's autograph is anybody's guess. No manuscript of any play in Shakespeare's handwriting has survived. Indeed, very few play manuscripts from this period by any author are extant. The Tudor and Stuart periods had not yet learned to prize autographs and authors' original manuscripts.

Since the First Folio contains eighteen plays not previously printed, it is the only source for these. For the other eighteen, which had appeared in quarto versions, the First Folio also has the authority of an edition prepared and overseen by Shakespeare's colleagues and professional associates. But since editorial standards in 1623 were far from strict, and Heminges and Condell were actors rather than editors by profession, the texts are sometimes careless. The printing and proofreading of the First Folio also left much to be desired, and some garbled passages have had to be corrected and emended. The "good quarto" texts have to be taken into account in preparing a modern edition.

Because of the great popularity of Shakespeare through the centuries, the First Folio has become a prized book, but it is not a very rare one, for it is estimated that 238 copies are extant. The Folger Shakespeare Library in Washington, D.C., has seventy-nine copies of the First Folio, collected by the founder, Henry Clay Folger, who believed that a collation of as many texts as possible would reveal significant facts about the text of Shakespeare's plays. Dr. Charlton Hinman, using an ingenious machine of his own invention for mechanical collating, has made many discoveries that throw light on Shakespeare's text and on printing practices of the day.

The probability is that the First Folio of 1623 had an edition of between 1,000 and 1,250 copies. It is believed that it sold for £1, which made it an expensive book, for £1 in 1623 was equivalent to something between $40 and $50 in modern purchasing power.

During the seventeenth century, Shakespeare was sufficiently popular to warrant three later editions in folio size, the Second Folio of 1632, the Third Folio of 1663–1664, and the Fourth Folio of 1685. The Third Folio added six other plays ascribed to Shakespeare, but these are apocryphal.

THE SHAKESPEAREAN THEATRE

The theatres in which Shakespeare's plays were performed were vastly different from those we know today. The stage was a platform that jutted out into the area now occupied by the first rows of seats on the main floor, what is called the "orchestra" in America and the "pit" in England. This platform had no curtain to come down at the ends of acts and scenes. And although simple stage properties were available, the Elizabethan theatre lacked both the machinery and the elaborate movable scenery of the modern theatre. In the rear of the platform stage was a curtained area that could be used as an inner room, a tomb, or any such scene that might be required. A balcony above this inner room, and perhaps balconies on the sides of the stage, could represent the upper deck of a ship, the entry to Juliet's room, or a prison window. A trap door in the stage provided an entrance for ghosts and devils from the nether regions, and a similar trap in the canopied structure over the stage, known as the "heavens," made it possible to let down angels on a rope. These primitive stage arrangements help to account for many elements in Elizabethan plays. For example, since there was no curtain, the dramatist frequently felt the necessity of writing into his play action to clear the stage at the ends of acts and scenes. The funeral march at the end of *Hamlet* is not there merely for atmosphere; Shakespeare had to get the corpses off the stage. The lack of scenery also freed the dramatist from undue concern about the exact location of his sets, and the physical relation of his various settings to each other did not have to be worked out with the same precision as in the modern theatre.

Before London had buildings designed exclusively for theatrical entertainment, plays were given in inns and taverns. The characteristic inn of the period had an inner courtyard with rooms opening onto balconies overlooking the yard. Players could set up their temporary stages at one end of the yard and audiences could find seats on the balconies out of the weather. The poorer sort could stand or sit on the cobblestones in the yard, which was open to the sky. The first theatres followed this construction, and throughout the Elizabethan period the large public theatres had a yard in front of the stage open to the weather, with two or three tiers of covered balconies extending around the theatre. This physical structure again influenced the writing of plays. Because a dramatist wanted the actors to be heard, he frequently wrote into his play orations that could be delivered with declamatory effect. He also provided spectacle, buffoonery, and broad jests to keep the riotous groundlings in the yard entertained and quiet.

In another respect the Elizabethan theatre differed greatly from ours. It had no actresses. All women's roles were taken by boys, sometimes recruited from the boys' choirs of the London churches. Some of these youths acted their roles with great skill and the Elizabethans did not seem to be aware of any incongruity. The first actresses on the professional English stage appeared after the Restoration of Charles II, in 1660, when exiled Englishmen brought back from France practices of the French stage.

London in the Elizabethan period, as now, was the center of theatrical interest, though wandering actors from time to time traveled through the country performing in inns, halls, and the houses of the nobility. The first professional playhouse, called simply The Theatre, was erected by James Burbage, father of Shakespeare's colleague, Richard Burbage, in 1576 on lands of the old Holywell Priory adjacent to Finsbury Fields, a playground and park area just north of the city walls. It had the advantage of being outside the city's jurisdiction and yet was near enough to be easily accessible. Soon after The Theatre was opened, another playhouse called The Curtain was erected in the same neighborhood. Both of these playhouses had open courtyards and were probably polygonal in shape.

About the time The Curtain opened, Richard Farrant, Master of the Children of the Chapel Royal at Windsor and of St. Paul's, conceived the idea of opening a "private" theatre in the old monastery buildings of the Blackfriars, not far from St. Paul's Cathedral in the heart of the city. This theatre was ostensibly to train the choirboys in plays for presentation at Court, but Farrant managed to present plays to paying audiences and achieved considerable success until aristocratic neighbors complained and had the theatre closed. The first Blackfriars Theatre was significant, however, because it popularized the boy actors in a professional way and it paved the way for a second theatre in the Blackfriars, which Shakespeare's company took over more than thirty years later. By the last years of the sixteenth century, London had at least six professional theatres and still others were erected during the reign of James I.

The Globe Theatre, the playhouse that most people connect with Shakespeare, was erected early in 1599 on the Bankside, the area across the Thames from the city. Its construction had a dramatic beginning, for on the night of December 28, 1598, James Burbage's sons, Cuthbert and Richard, gathered together a crew who tore down the old theatre in Holywell and carted the timbers across the river to a site that they had chosen for a new playhouse. The reason for this clandestine operation was a row with the landowner over the lease to the Holywell property. The site chosen for the Globe was another playground outside of the city's jurisdiction, a region of somewhat unsavory character. Not far away was the Bear Garden, an amphitheatre devoted to the baiting of bears and bulls. This was also the region occupied by many houses of ill fame licensed by the Bishop of Winchester and the source of substantial revenue to him. But it was easily accessible either from London Bridge or by means of the cheap boats operated by the London watermen, and it had the great advantage of being beyond the authority of the Puritanical aldermen of London, who frowned on plays because they lured apprentices from work, filled their heads with improper ideas, and generally exerted a bad influence. The aldermen also complained that the crowds drawn together in the theatre helped to spread the plague.

The Globe was the handsomest theatre up to its time. It was a large building, apparently octagonal in shape, and open like its predecessors to the sky in the center, but capable of seating a large audience in its covered balconies. To erect and operate the Globe, the Burbages organized a syndicate composed of the leading members of the dramatic company, of which Shakespeare was a member. Since it was open to the weather and depended on natural light, plays had to be given in the afternoon. This caused no hardship in the long afternoons of an English summer, but in the winter the weather was a great handicap and discouraged all except the hardiest. For that reason, in 1608 Shakespeare's company was glad to take over the lease of the second

Blackfriars Theatre, a substantial, roomy hall reconstructed within the framework of the old monastery building. This theatre was protected from the weather and its stage was artificially lighted by chandeliers of candles. This became the winter playhouse for Shakespeare's company and at once proved so popular that the congestion of traffic created an embarrassing problem. Stringent regulations had to be made for the movement of coaches in the vicinity. Shakespeare's company continued to use the Globe during the summer months. In 1613 a squib fired from a cannon during a performance of *Henry VIII* fell on the thatched roof and the Globe burned to the ground. The next year it was rebuilt.

London had other famous theatres. The Rose, just west of the Globe, was built by Philip Henslowe, a semiliterate denizen of the Bankside, who became one of the most important theatrical owners and producers of the Tudor and Stuart periods. What is more important for historians, he kept a detailed account book, which provides much of our information about theatrical history in his time. Another famous theatre on the Bankside was the Swan, which a Dutch priest, Johannes de Witt, visited in 1596. The crude drawing of the stage which he made was copied by his friend Arend van Buchell; it is one of the important pieces of contemporary evidence for theatrical construction. Among the other theatres, the Fortune, north of the city, on Golding Lane, and the Red Bull, even farther away from the city, off St. John's Street, were the most popular. The

Red Bull, much frequented by apprentices, favored sensational and sometimes rowdy plays.

The actors who kept all of these theatres going were organized into companies under the protection of some noble patron. Traditionally actors had enjoyed a low reputation. In some of the ordinances they were classed as vagrants; in the phraseology of the time, "rogues, vagabonds, sturdy beggars, and common players" were all listed together as undesirables. To escape penalties often meted out to these characters, organized groups of actors managed to gain the protection of various personages of high degree. In the later years of Elizabeth's reign, a group flourished under the name of the Queen's Men; another group had the protection of the Lord Admiral and were known as the Lord Admiral's Men. Edward Alleyn, son-in-law of Philip Henslowe, was the leading spirit in the Lord Admiral's Men. Besides the adult companies, troupes of boy actors from time to time also enjoyed considerable popularity. Among these were the Children of Paul's and the Children of the Chapel Royal.

The company with which Shakespeare had a long association had for its first patron Henry Carey, Lord Hunsdon, the Lord Chamberlain, and hence they were known as the Lord Chamberlain's Men. After the accession of James I, they became the King's Men. This company was the great rival of the Lord Admiral's Men, managed by Henslowe and Alleyn.

All was not easy for the players in Shakespeare's time, for the aldermen of London were always eager for an excuse to close up the Blackfriars and any other theatres in their jurisdiction. The theatres outside the jurisdiction of London were not immune from interference, for they might be shut up by order of the Privy Council for meddling in politics or for various other offenses, or they might be closed in time of plague lest they spread infection. During plague times, the actors usually went on tour and played the provinces wherever they could find an audience. Particularly frightening were the plagues of 1592–1594 and 1613 when the theatres closed and the players, like many other Londoners, had to take to the country.

Though players had a low social status, they enjoyed great popularity, and one of the favorite forms of entertainment at Court was the performance of plays. To be commanded to perform at Court conferred great prestige upon a company of players, and printers frequently noted that fact when they published plays. Several of Shakespeare's plays were performed before the sovereign, and Shakespeare himself undoubtedly acted in some of these plays.

REFERENCES FOR FURTHER READING

Many readers will want suggestions for further reading about Shakespeare and his times. A few references will serve as guides to further study in the enormous literature on the subject. A simple and useful little book is Gerald Sanders, *A Shakespeare Primer* (New York, 1950). *A Companion to Shake-*

speare Studies, edited by Harley Granville-Barker and G. B. Harrison (Cambridge, 1934), is a valuable guide. The most recent concise handbook of facts about Shakespeare is Gerald E. Bentley, *Shakespeare: A Biographical Handbook* (New Haven, 1961). More detailed but not so voluminous as to be confusing is Hazelton Spencer, *The Art and Life of William Shakespeare* (New York, 1940), which, like Sanders' and Bentley's handbooks, contains a brief annotated list of useful books on various aspects of the subject. The most detailed and scholarly work providing complete factual information about Shakespeare is Sir Edmund Chambers, *William Shakespeare: A Study of Facts and Problems* (2 vols., Oxford, 1930). A vast amount of general information about a wide variety of Shakespearean material is to be found in *The Reader's Encyclopedia of Shakespeare*, edited by O. J. Campbell and Edward G. Quinn (New York, 1966).

Among other biographies of Shakespeare, Joseph Quincy Adams, *A Life of William Shakespeare* (Boston, 1923) is still an excellent assessment of the essential facts and the traditional information, and Marchette Chute, *Shakespeare of London* (New York, 1949; paperback, 1957) stresses Shakespeare's life in the theatre. Two new biographies of Shakespeare have recently appeared. A. L. Rowse, *William Shakespeare: A Biography* (London, 1963; New York, 1964) provides an appraisal by a distinguished English historian, who dismisses the notion that somebody else wrote Shakespeare's plays as arrant nonsense that runs counter to known historical fact.

Peter Quennell, *Shakespeare: A Biography* (Cleveland and New York, 1963) is a sensitive and intelligent survey of what is known and surmised of Shakespeare's life. Louis B. Wright, *Shakespeare for Everyman* (New York, 1964; 1965) discusses the basis of Shakespeare's enduring popularity.

The *Shakespeare Quarterly*, published by the Shakespeare Association of America under the editorship of James G. McManaway, is recommended for those who wish to keep up with current Shakespearean scholarship and stage productions. The *Quarterly* includes an annual bibliography of Shakespeare editions and works on Shakespeare published during the previous year.

The question of the authenticity of Shakespeare's plays arouses perennial attention. The theory of hidden cryptograms in the plays is demolished by William F. and Elizebeth S. Friedman, *The Shakespearean Ciphers Examined* (New York, 1957). A succinct account of the various absurdities advanced to suggest the authorship of a multitude of candidates other than Shakespeare will be found in R. C. Churchill, *Shakespeare and His Betters* (Bloomington, Ind., 1959). Another recent discussion of the subject, *The Authorship of Shakespeare*, by James G. McManaway (Washington, D.C., 1962), presents the evidence from contemporary records to prove the identity of Shakespeare the actor-playwright with Shakespeare of Stratford.

Scholars are not in agreement about the details of playhouse construction in the Elizabethan period. John C. Adams presents a plausible reconstruction of the Globe in *The Globe Playhouse: Its Design and Equipment* (Cambridge, Mass., 1942; 2nd rev. ed., 1961). A description with excellent drawings based on Dr. Adams' model is Irwin Smith, *Shakespeare's Globe Playhouse: A Modern Reconstruction in Text and Scale Drawings* (New York, 1956). Other sensible discussions are C. Walter Hodges, *The Globe Restored* (London, 1953) and A. M. Nagler, *Shakespeare's Stage* (New Haven, 1958). Bernard Beckerman, *Shakespeare at the Globe, 1599–1609* (New Haven, 1962; paperback, 1962) discusses Elizabethan staging and acting techniques.

A sound and readable history of the early theatres is Joseph Quincy Adams, *Shakespearean Playhouses: A History of English Theatres from the Beginnings to the Restoration* (Boston, 1917). For detailed, factual information about the Elizabethan and seventeenth-century stages, the definitive reference works are Sir Edmund Chambers, *The Elizabethan Stage* (4 vols., Oxford, 1923) and Gerald E. Bentley, *The Jacobean and Caroline Stages* (5 vols., Oxford, 1941–1956).

Further information on the history of the theatre and related topics will be found in the following titles: T. W. Baldwin, *The Organization and Personnel of the Shakespearean Company* (Princeton, 1927); Lily Bess Campbell, *Scenes and Machines on the English Stage during the Renaissance* (Cambridge, 1923); Esther Cloudman Dunn, *Shakespeare in America* (New York, 1939); George C. D. Odell, *Shakespeare from Betterton to Irving* (2 vols., London, 1931); Arthur Colby Sprague, *Shakespeare and the Actors: The Stage Business in His Plays (1660–1905)* (Cambridge, Mass., 1944) and *Shakespearian Players and Performances* (Cambridge, Mass., 1953); Leslie Hotson, *The Commonwealth and Restoration Stage* (Cambridge, Mass., 1928); Alwin Thaler, *Shakspere to Sheridan: A Book about the Theatre of Yesterday and To-day* (Cambridge, Mass., 1922); George C. Branam, *Eighteenth-Century Adaptations of Shakespeare's Tragedies* (Berkeley, 1956); C. Beecher Hogan, *Shakespeare in the Theatre, 1701–1800* (Oxford, 1957); Ernest Bradlee Watson, *Sheridan to Robertson: A Study of the 19th-Century London Stage* (Cambridge, Mass., 1926); and Enid Welsford, *The Court Masque* (Cambridge, Mass., 1927).

A brief account of the growth of Shakespeare's reputation is F. E. Halliday, *The Cult of Shakespeare* (London, 1947). A more detailed discussion is given in Augustus Ralli, *A History of Shakespearian Criticism* (2 vols., Oxford, 1932; New York, 1958). Harley Granville-Barker, *Prefaces to Shakespeare* (5 vols., London, 1927–1948; 2 vols., London, 1958) provides stimulating critical discussion of the plays. An older classic of criticism is Andrew C. Bradley, *Shakespearean Tragedy: Lectures on Hamlet, Othello, King Lear, Macbeth* (London, 1904; paperback, 1955). Sir Edmund Chambers, *Shakespeare: A Survey* (London, 1935; paperback, 1958) contains short, sensible essays on thirty-four of the plays, originally written as introductions to single-play editions. Alfred Harbage, *William Shakespeare: A Reader's Guide* (New York, 1963) is a handbook to the reading and appreciation of the plays, with scene synopses and interpretation.

For the history plays see Lily Bess Campbell, *Shakespeare's "Histories": Mirrors of Elizabethan Policy* (Cambridge, 1947); John Palmer, *Political Characters of Shakespeare* (London, 1945; 1961); E. M. W. Tillyard, *Shakespeare's History Plays* (London, 1948); Irving Ribner, *The English History Play in the Age of Shakespeare* (Princeton, 1947; rev. ed., New York, 1965); Max M. Reese, *The Cease of Majesty* (London, 1961; New York, 1962); and Arthur Colby Sprague, *Shakespeare's Histories: Plays for the Stage* (London, 1964). Harold Jenkins, "Shakespeare's History Plays: 1900–1951," *Shakespeare Survey 6* (Cambridge, 1953), 1–15, provides an excellent survey of recent critical opinion on the subject.

Pericles, aside from studies of the problem of authorship, has inspired relatively little commentary. Both authorship and sources are fully discussed in Bullough's *Narrative and Dramatic Sources of Shakespeare*, VI, *Other "Classical" Plays* (London and New York, 1966) and in the new Arden edition of *Pericles*, edited by F. D. Hoeniger (London and Cambridge, Mass., 1963).

The comedies are illuminated by the following studies: C. L. Barber, *Shakespeare's Festive Comedy* (Princeton, 1959); John Russell Brown, *Shakespeare and His Comedies* (London, 1957); H. B. Charlton, *Shakespearian Comedy* (London, 1938; 4th ed., 1949); W. W. Lawrence, *Shakespeare's Problem*

Comedies (New York, 1931); and Thomas M. Parrott, *Shakespearean Comedy* (New York, 1949).

Further discussions of Shakespeare's tragedies, in addition to Bradley, already cited, are contained in H. B. Charlton, *Shakespearian Tragedy* (Cambridge, 1948); Willard Farnham, *The Medieval Heritage of Elizabethan Tragedy* (Berkeley, 1936) and *Shakespeare's Tragic Frontier: The World of His Final Tragedies* (Berkeley, 1950); and Harold S. Wilson, *On the Design of Shakespearian Tragedy* (Toronto, 1957).

The "Roman" plays are treated in M. M. MacCallum, *Shakespeare's Roman Plays and Their Background* (London, 1910) and J. C. Maxwell, "Shakespeare's Roman Plays, 1900–1956," *Shakespeare Survey 10* (Cambridge, 1957), 1–11.

Kenneth Muir, *Shakespeare's Sources: Comedies and Tragedies* (London, 1957) discusses Shakespeare's use of source material. The sources themselves have been reprinted several times. Among old editions are John P. Collier (ed.), *Shakespeare's Library* (2 vols., London, 1850), Israel C. Gollancz (ed.), *The Shakespeare Classics* (12 vols., London, 1907–1926), and W. C. Hazlitt (ed.), *Shakespeare's Library* (6 vols., London, 1875). A modern edition is being prepared by Geoffrey Bullough with the title *Narrative and Dramatic Sources of Shakespeare* (London and New York, 1957–). Six volumes, covering all the plays except the tragedies, have been published to date (1967).

In addition to the second edition of *Webster's New International Dictionary*, which contains most of the unusual words used by Shakespeare, the following reference works are helpful: Edwin A. Abbott, *A Shakespearian Grammar* (London, 1872; paperback, 1966); C. T. Onions, *A Shakespeare Glossary* (2nd rev. ed., Oxford, 1925); and Eric Partridge, *Shakespeare's Bawdy* (New York, 1948; paperback, 1960).

Some knowledge of the social background of the period in which Shakespeare lived is important for a full understanding of his work. A brief, clear, and accurate account of Tudor history is S. T. Bindoff, *The Tudors*, in the Penguin series. A readable general history is G. M. Trevelyan, *The History of England*, first published in 1926 and available in numerous editions. The same author's *English Social History*, first published in 1942 and also available in many editions, provides fascinating information about England in all periods. Sir John Neale, *Queen Elizabeth* (London, 1935; paperback, 1957) is the best study of the great Queen. Various aspects of life in the Elizabethan period are treated in Louis B. Wright, *Middle-Class Culture in Elizabethan England* (Chapel Hill, N.C., 1935; reprinted Ithaca, N.Y., 1958, 1964). *Shakespeare's England: An Account of the Life and Manners of His Age*, edited by Sidney Lee and C. T. Onions (2 vols., Oxford, 1917), provides much information on many aspects of Elizabethan life. A fascinating survey of the period will be found in Muriel St. C. Byrne, *Elizabethan Life in Town and Country* (London, 1925; rev. ed., 1954; paperback, 1961).

The Folger Library is issuing a series of illustrated

booklets entitled "Folger Booklets on Tudor and Stuart Civilization," printed and distributed by Cornell University Press. Published to date are the following titles:

D. W. Davies, *Dutch Influences on English Culture, 1558–1625*

Giles E. Dawson, *The Life of William Shakespeare*

Ellen C. Eyler, *Early English Gardens and Garden Books*

Elaine W. Fowler, *English Sea Power in the Early Tudor Period, 1485–1558*

John R. Hale, *The Art of War and Renaissance England*

William Haller, *Elizabeth I and the Puritans*

Virginia A. LaMar, *English Dress in the Age of Shakespeare*

————, *Travel and Roads in England*

John L. Lievsay, *The Elizabethan Image of Italy*

James G. McManaway, *The Authorship of Shakespeare*

Dorothy E. Mason, *Music in Elizabethan England*

Garrett Mattingly, *The "Invincible" Armada and Elizabethan England*

Boies Penrose, *Tudor and Early Stuart Voyaging*

T. I. Rae, *Scotland in the Time of Shakespeare*

Conyers Read, *The Government of England under Elizabeth*

Albert J. Schmidt, *The Yeoman in Tudor and Stuart England*

Lilly C. Stone, *English Sports and Recreations*

At intervals the Folger Library plans to gather these booklets in hardbound volumes. The first is *Life and Letters in Tudor and Stuart England, First Folger Series*, edited by Louis B. Wright and Virginia A. LaMar (published for the Folger Shakespeare Library by Cornell University Press, 1962). The volume contains eleven of the separate booklets.

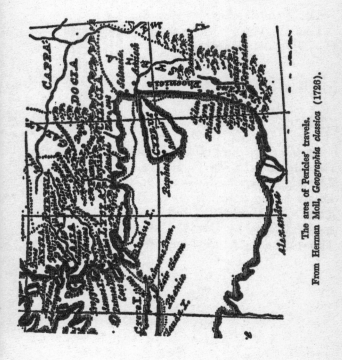

The area of Pericles' travels.
From Herman Moll, *Geographia classica* (1726).

[Dramatis Personae*

Antiochus, King of Antioch.
Pericles, Prince of Tyre.
Helicanus,
Escanes, } two lords of Tyre.
Simonides, King of Pentapolis.
Cleon, Governor of Tarsus.
Lysimachus, Governor of Mytilene.
Cerimon, a lord of Ephesus.
Thaliard, a lord of Antioch.
Philemon, servant to *Cerimon*.
Leonine, servant to *Dionyza*.
Marshal.
A pander.
Boult, his servant.

The daughter of Antiochus.
Dionyza, wife to *Cleon*.
Thaisa, daughter to *Simonides*.
Marina, daughter to *Pericles* and *Thaisa*.
Lychorida, nurse to *Marina*.
A bawd.
Lords, Knights, Gentlemen, Sailors, Pirates, Fishermen,
and Messengers.

Diana.

Gower, as Chorus.

SCENE: *Various Mediterranean countries*.]

*First printed as "The Actors' Names" in the Third Folio but cor-
rected by later editors.

PERICLES

PRINCE OF TYRE

ACT I

[I.Pro.] Gower, as Prologue, relates how Antiochus, King of Tyre, has seduced his own daughter and devised a plan to get rid of all suitors for her hand.

<hr/>

2. ancient Gower: the poet John Gower, whose *Confessio Amantis,* one of the sources for this play, was written in the fourteenth century and first printed by William Caxton in 1483.

3. man's infirmities: i.e., those of the flesh.

6. Ember Eves: the evenings before Ember Days, periods of fasting fixed by the Church; **holy ales:** more commonly called "church ales," religious festivals at which ale was drunk liberally.

8. restoratives: i.e., inspiration.

9. purchase: beneficial result; **glorious:** eager for glory; full of lofty aspiration.

10. Et bonum quo antiquius, eo melius: and the older a good thing, the better.

12. wit's more ripe: learning is more advanced.

16. Waste it for you like taper light: proverbial; compare "A candle lights others and consumes itself."

17. Antioch: modern Antakya, in Turkey; **Antiochus the Great:** historically, Antiochus III, King of Syria, 223–187 B.C.

[ACT I]

[Before the Palace of Antioch.]

Enter Gower [as Prologue].

To sing a song that old was sung,
From ashes ancient Gower is come,
Assuming man's infirmities,
To glad your ear and please your eyes.
It hath been sung at festivals,   5
On Ember Eves and holy ales;
And lords and ladies in their lives
Have read it for restoratives.
The purchase is to make men glorious,
Et bonum quo antiquius, eo melius.   10
If you, born in these latter times,
When wit's more ripe, accept my rhymes,
And that to hear an old man sing
May to your wishes pleasure bring,
I life would wish and that I might   15
Waste it for you like taper light.
This Antioch, then, Antiochus the Great
Built up, this city, for his chiefest seat,
The fairest in all Syria.
I tell you what mine authors say: 20

1

21. **peer:** mate.

23. **buxom:** amiable; gracious; **full of face:** beautiful.

24. **As:** as though.

32. **frame:** direct themselves.

36. **keep her still and men in awe:** retain possession of her always and keep other men at a distance.

39. **wight:** fellow.

40. **yon grim looks:** the heads of other unsuccessful suitors, which Antiochus had placed on the castle gates, according to Wilkins' novel.

42. **my cause who best can justify:** who can best vouch for the truth of this relation by seeing it acted out.

▬▬▬▬▬▬▬▬▬▬▬▬▬▬▬▬▬▬▬▬

[I.i.] Pericles, Prince of Tyre, ventures to win the hand of Antiochus' daughter by explaining a riddle. If he fails to answer correctly, he will lose his head, and Antiochus seeks to discourage him by pointing out the skulls of suitors who have failed. Pericles is charmed by the beauty of Antiochus' daughter, but he correctly interprets the riddle as a revelation of her incestuous relationship with her father. Although Pericles dares not expound the riddle, Antiochus perceives that he has guessed the truth. He urges Pericles to delay in answering and promises him sumptuous entertainment. Secretly he plans to have Pericles murdered, but the latter, distrusting his intentions, flees.

▬▬▬▬▬▬▬▬▬▬▬▬▬▬▬▬▬▬▬▬

1-2. **at large received:** been fully informed of.

2

This king unto him took a peer,
Who died and left a female heir,
So buxom, blithe, and full of face
As Heaven had lent her all His grace;
With whom the father liking took 25
And her to incest did provoke.
Bad child, worse father! To entice his own
To evil should be done by none.
But custom what they did begin
Was with long use accounted no sin. 30
The beauty of this sinful dame
Made many princes thither frame
To seek her as a bedfellow,
In marriage pleasures playfellow:
Which to prevent he made a law, 35
To keep her still and men in awe,
That whoso asked her for his wife,
His riddle told not, lost his life.
So for her many a wight did die,
As yon grim looks do testify. 40
What now ensues, to the judgment of your eye
I give, my cause who best can justify.

Exit.

[Scene I. Antioch. A room in the palace.]

Enter Antiochus, Prince Pericles, and Followers.

Ant. Young Prince of Tyre, you have at large received

10. **Lucina:** a name for the Roman goddess Juno as protectress of women in childbirth; **till Lucina reigned** therefore means until her mother gave birth to her.

11. **glad her presence:** make her charming.

15. **Graces her subjects:** figuratively, "attended by the Graces of classical mythology," who were associated with Spring; literally, "mistress of every grace." The image recalls Botticelli's famous "Primavera."

16. **gives:** that gives.

17. **book of praises:** compendium of all that is praiseworthy.

18. **curious:** exquisite.

20. **her mild companion:** i.e., the companion of one so mild.

26. **compass:** achieve.

29. **Hesperides:** in the list of "the Actors' Names" at the end of the play in the Third Folio, Antiochus' daughter is so named. Most editors assume this to be an editorial misconstruction of Antiochus' words, but Pericles likens her to a precious tree in line 23, and it is possible that the author meant her to be called Hesperides. In classical mythology, the Hesperides were the daughters of Hesperus. One of Hercules' labors was to steal some fruit from a tree in their garden. Many Elizabethan writers seem to have thought that the garden itself was called the Hesperides.

The danger of the task you undertake.
   Per. I have, Antiochus, and, with a soul
Emboldened with the glory of her praise,   5
Think death no hazard in this enterprise.
   Ant. Music!   [*Music plays.*]
Bring in our daughter, clothed like a bride,
For the embracements even of Jove himself;
At whose conception, till Lucina reigned,   10
Nature this dowry gave: to glad her presence,
The senate house of planets all did sit,
To knit in her their best perfections.

Enter Antiochus' Daughter.

   Per. See where she comes, appareled like the Spring,
Graces her subjects, and her thoughts the king   15
Of every virtue gives renown to men!
Her face the book of praises, where is read
Nothing but curious pleasures, as from thence
Sorrow were ever razed and testy wrath
Could never be her mild companion.   20
You gods that made me man and sway in love,
That have inflamed desire in my breast
To taste the fruit of yon celestial tree
Or die in the adventure, be my helps,
As I am son and servant to your will,   25
To compass such a boundless happiness!
   Ant. Prince Pericles—
   Per. That would be son to great Antiochus.
   Ant. Before thee stands this fair Hesperides,
With golden fruit, but dangerous to be touched;   30

31. **dragons:** according to some mythographers, the dragon Ladon guarded the tree.

35. **all thy whole heap:** your whole body.

36. **sometimes:** formerly, referring to the heads of the suitors who have failed.

43. **For:** for fear of; **going on:** walking into.

48. **Death remembered should be like a mirror:** i.e., recalling the image of Death should warn us that "to this favor" we must come, as Hamlet put it (V i, 187).

49. **breath:** i.e., something brief and insubstantial.

51. **know the world:** are schooled in worldly values.

52. **Gripe:** clutch; **erst:** formerly.

59. **conclusion:** problem (the riddle).

"Death remembered should be like a mirror."
From Richard Turnbull, *An Exposition upon the Canonical Epistle of Saint Jude* (1606).

4

For death, like dragons, here affright thee hard.
Her face, like Heaven, enticeth thee to view
Her countless glory, which desert must gain;
And which, without desert, because thine eye
Presumes to reach, all thy whole heap must die. 35
Yon sometimes famous princes, like thyself,
Drawn by report, advent'rous by desire,
Tell thee, with speechless tongues and semblance
    pale,
That without covering, save yon field of stars, 40
Here they stand martyrs, slain in Cupid's wars;
And with dead cheeks advise thee to desist
For going on Death's net, whom none resist.
   Per. Antiochus, I thank thee, who hath taught
My frail mortality to know itself 45
And by those fearful objects to prepare
This body, like to them, to what I must;
For Death remembered should be like a mirror,
Who tells us life's but breath, to trust it error.
I'll make my will then, and, as sick men do, 50
Who know the world, see Heaven, but feeling woe
Gripe not at earthly joys as erst they did,
So I bequeath a happy peace to you
And all good men, as every prince should do;
My riches to the earth from whence they came; 55
But my unspotted fire of love to you [*To the Princess*].
Thus ready for the way of life or death,
I wait the sharpest blow, Antiochus.
   Ant. Scorning advice, read the conclusion then:
Which read and not expounded, 'tis decreed, 60
As these before thee thou thyself shalt bleed.

62. **'sayed yet:** i.e., who have assayed so far to explain the riddle.

76. **Sharp physic is the last:** the last line threatens a bitter medicine—death.

80. **Fair glass of light:** one whose radiant beauty blinds the viewer to her inner ugliness.

83. **on whom perfections wait:** attended by virtues.

91. **Good sooth:** verily.

Pseudo-classical dress, typical of romances.
From *Le premier livre d'Amadis de Gaule* (1555).

Ant. He hath found the meaning, for which we
   mean
To have his head.
He must not live to trumpet forth my infamy,
Nor tell the world Antiochus doth sin   155
In such a loathed manner:
And therefore instantly this Prince must die,
For by his fall my honor must keep high.
Who attends us there?

Enter Thaliard.

Thal. Doth your Highness call?   160
Ant. Thaliard,
You are of our chamber, Thaliard, and our mind
   partakes
Her private actions to your secrecy;
And for your faithfulness we will advance you.   165
Thaliard, behold, here's poison, and here's gold.
We hate the Prince of Tyre, and thou must kill him.
It fits thee not to ask the reason why,
Because we bid it. Say, is it done?
Thal.   My lord,   170
'Tis done.
Ant. Enough.

Enter a Messenger.

Let your breath cool yourself, telling your haste.
Mess. My lord, Prince Pericles is fled.   [*Exit.*]
Ant.   As thou   175

178. **level:** aim.

178. **My heart can lend no succor to my head:** my heart (courage) cannot relieve my anxious mind.

[I.ii.] Back in Tyre, Pericles broods over his fear of Antiochus. The Lord Helicanus, a trusted counselor, persuades him to reveal his trouble. Agreeing that Pericles' life is in danger from Antiochus, he advises the Prince to travel until Antiochus has either relented or died. Pericles agrees and announces his intention of going to Tarsus, leaving Helicanus to govern Tyre in his absence.

---

4. **used:** familiar.

11. **arm:** see the proverb "Kings have long arms."

Wilt live, fly after; and like an arrow shot
From a well-experienced archer hits the mark
His eye doth level at, so thou ne'er return
Unless thou say Prince Pericles is dead.
 Thal. My lord,   **180**
If I can get him within my pistol's length,
I'll make him sure enough: so, farewell to your Highness.
 Ant. Thaliard, adieu! [*Exit Thaliard.*] Till Pericles
  be dead,   **185**
My heart can lend no succor to my head.

              Exit.

[Scene II. Tyre. A room in the palace.]

Enter Pericles with his Lords.

 Per. Let none disturb us.   [*Exeunt Lords.*]
      Why should this change of thoughts,
The sad companion, dull-eyed melancholy,
Be my so used a guest as not an hour
In the day's glorious walk or peaceful night, **5**
The tomb where grief should sleep, can breed me
  quiet?
Here pleasures court mine eyes, and mine eyes shun
  them,
And danger, which I feared, is at Antioch, **10**
Whose arm seems far too short to hit me here:

14. **passions:** disturbances.
15. **misdread:** dread of evil.
16. **care:** nursing.
18. **cares:** takes care.
23. **boots:** avails.
28. **ostent:** show; **huge:** threatening.
29. **Amazement:** terror.
34. **fence:** shelter.

"The tops of trees, which fence the roots they grow by
and defend them." A symbol of Charity.
From Cesare Ripa, *Iconologia* (1603).

Yet neither pleasure's art can joy my spirits,
Nor yet the other's distance comfort me.
Then it is thus: the passions of the mind,
That have their first conception by misdread,   15
Have after-nourishment and life by care;
And what was first but fear what might be done,
Grows elder now and cares it be not done.
And so with me: the great Antiochus,
'Gainst whom I am too little to contend,   20
Since he's so great can make his will his act,
Will think me speaking, though I swear to silence;
Nor boots it me to say I honor him,
If he suspect I may dishonor him.
And what may make him blush in being known,   25
He'll stop the course by which it might be known.
With hostile forces he'll o'erspread the land,
And with the ostent of war will look so huge,
Amazement shall drive courage from the state,
Our men be vanquished ere they do resist,   30
And subjects punished that ne'er thought offense:
Which care of them, not pity of myself—
Who am no more but as the tops of trees
Which fence the roots they grow by and defend
    them—   35
Makes both my body pine and soul to languish,
And punish that before that he would punish.

Enter [Helicanus,] and all the other Lords to Pericles.

    1. Lord. Joy and all comfort in your sacred breast!

39. till you return to us: Pericles has not yet decided to leave Tyre. Editors generally have found the continuity of this scene baffling and conclude that some dialogue may have been inadvertently omitted in the copy or by the printer.

41. give: allow.

42. abuse: wrong.

48. Signior Sooth: Sir Soothe (Flatter).

52. o'erlook: examine.

   2. Lord. And keep your mind, till you return to us,
Peaceful and comfortable!   40
   Hel. Peace, peace, and give experience tongue.
They do abuse the king that flatter him.
For flattery is the bellows blows up sin;
The thing the which is flattered but a spark,
To which that blast gives heat and stronger glowing;   45
Whereas reproof, obedient and in order,
Fits kings, as they are men, for they may err.
When Signior Sooth here does proclaim a peace,
He flatters you, makes war upon your life.
Prince, pardon me, or strike me, if you please;   50
I cannot be much lower than my knees.   [*Kneeling.*]
   Per. All leave us else; but let your cares o'erlook
What shipping and what lading's in our haven,
And then return to us.   [*Exeunt Lords.*]
                     Helicanus, thou   55
Hast moved us. What seest thou in our looks?
   Hel. An angry brow, dread lord.
   Per. If there be such a dart in princes' frowns,
How durst thy tongue move anger to our face?
   Hel. How dares the plants look up to Heaven, from   60
    whence
They have their nourishment?
   Per.   Thou knowst I have power
To take thy life from thee.
   Hel. I have ground the axe myself;   65
Do but you strike the blow.
   Per. Rise, prithee, rise. Sit down. Thou art no flat-
    terer: [*Helicanus rises.*]

81. **purchase:** gain.
82. **issue:** heir, or heirs.
83. **Are:** i.e., such as are.
87. **smooth:** speak graciously but insincerely.
90. **careful:** protective.
92. **succeed:** ensue.
95. **doubt it:** fear it.
98. **unlaid ope:** unrevealed.

I thank thee for't; and Heaven forbid
That kings should let their ears hear their faults hid! 70
Fit counselor and servant for a prince,
Who by thy wisdom makes a prince thy servant,
What wouldst thou have me do?
   Hel.   To bear with patience
Such griefs as you yourself do lay upon yourself. 75
   Per. Thou speakst like a physician, Helicanus,
That ministers a potion unto me
That thou wouldst tremble to receive thyself.
Attend me then: I went to Antioch,
Where, as thou knowst, against the face of death, 80
I sought the purchase of a glorious beauty
From whence an issue I might propagate
Are arms to princes and bring joys to subjects.
Her face was to mine eye beyond all wonder;
The rest—hark in thine ear—as black as incest: 85
Which by my knowledge found, the sinful father
Seemed not to strike but smooth: but thou knowst this,
'Tis time to fear when tyrants seems to kiss.
Which fear so grew in me, I hither fled,
Under the covering of a careful night, 90
Who seemed my good protector; and, being here,
Bethought me what was past, what might succeed.
I knew him tyrannous; and tyrants' fears
Decrease not but grow faster than the years.
And should he doubt it, as no doubt he doth, 95
That I should open to the list'ning air
How many worthy princes' bloods were shed
To keep his bed of blackness unlaid ope,
To lop that doubt, he'll fill this land with arms

101. **for mine, if I may call offense:** for my offense, if so I may call it.

120. **the Destinies:** the classical Fates; see cut.

128. **Intend:** direct.

129. **dispose myself:** adjust my behavior.

The Destinies, or Fates.
From Vincenzo Cartari, *Imagini de i dei de gli antichi* (1587).

And make pretense of wrong that I have done him;   100
When all, for mine, if I may call offense,
Must feel war's blow, who spares not innocence:
Which love to all, of which thyself art one,
Who now reprovedst me for't—
   Hel.   Alas, sir!   105
   Per. Drew sleep out of mine eyes, blood from my
      cheeks,
Musing into my mind, with thousand doubts
How I might stop this tempest ere it came;
And finding little comfort to relieve them,   110
I thought it princely charity to grieve them.
   Hel. Well, my lord, since you have given me leave
      to speak,
Freely will I speak. Antiochus you fear;
And justly, too, I think, you fear the tyrant,   115
Who either by public war or private treason
Will take away your life.
Therefore, my lord, go travel for a while,
Till that his rage and anger be forgot,
Or till the Destinies do cut his thread of life.   120
Your rule direct to any; if to me,
Day serves not light more faithful than I'll be.
   Per. I do not doubt thy faith;
But should he wrong my liberties in my absence?
   Hel. We'll mingle our bloods together in the earth,   125
From whence we had our being and our birth.
   Per. Tyre, I now look from thee, then, and to Tarsus
Intend my travel, where I'll hear from thee;
And by whose letters I'll dispose myself.
The care I had and have of subjects' good   130

134. **orbs:** orbits; **so round and safe:** in so straightforward and trustworthy a manner.

135. **of both:** i.e., Helicanus and himself; **convince:** overcome.

136. **a subject's shine, I a true prince:** i.e., the noble behavior (glory) becoming to a loyal subject, while I behaved like a true monarch. Comparison of the monarch to the sun and his attendants to lesser luminaries was common.

_____

[I.iii.] Thaliard arrives in Tyre with a commission from King Antiochus to murder Pericles. When he learns that Pericles has gone to sea, he believes that Antiochus will be satisfied by the possibility that Pericles' death will be inevitable.

_____

4. **a wise fellow:** the poet Philippides, who, in Plutarch's *Lives*, was asked by King Lysimachus what gift he would like and replied anything, provided that the King give him none of his secrets.

8. **indenture:** contract of service.

On thee I lay, whose wisdom's strength can bear it.
I'll take thy word for faith, not ask thine oath.
Who shuns not to break one will sure crack both:
But in our orbs we'll live so round and safe,
That time of both this truth shall ne'er convince, 135
Thou showedst a subject's shine, I a true prince.

Exeunt.

[Scene III. Tyre. An antechamber in the palace.]

Enter Thaliard solus.

Thal. So, this is Tyre and this the court. Here must
I kill King Pericles; and if I do it not, I am sure to be
hanged at home: 'tis dangerous. Well, I perceive he
was a wise fellow and had good discretion that, being
bid to ask what he would of the king, desired he might 5
know none of his secrets. Now do I see he had some
reason for't; for if a king bid a man be a villain, he's
bound by the indenture of his oath to be one. Husht!
here come the lords of Tyre.

Enter Helicanus, Escanes, with other Lords.

Hel. You shall not need, my fellow peers of Tyre, 10
Further to question me of your king's departure.
His sealed commission left in trust with me
Does speak sufficiently he's gone to travel.
Thal. [*Aside*] How! the King gone!

16. **unlicensed of your loves:** without your loving permission.

22. **doubting:** fearing.

27. **although I would:** even if I wished to be.

28. **the King's ears it must please:** i.e., the King must be pleased by being assured that.

38. **Commended:** offered.

Hel. If further yet you will be satisfied,   15
Why, as it were unlicensed of your loves,
He would depart, I'll give some light unto you.
Being at Antioch—
   Thal. [*Aside*]   What from Antioch?
   Hel. Royal Antiochus—on what cause I know not—   20
Took some displeasure at him; at least he judged so:
And doubting lest that he had erred or sinned,
To show his sorrow, he'd correct himself;
So puts himself unto the shipman's toil,
With whom each minute threatens life or death.   25
   Thal. [*Aside*] Well, I perceive
I shall not be hanged now, although I would;
But since he's gone, the King's ears it must please
He 'scaped the land, to perish at the sea.
I'll present myself. Peace to the lords of Tyre!   30
   Hel. Lord Thaliard from Antiochus is welcome.
   Thal. From him I come
With message unto princely Pericles;
But, since my landing I have understood
Your lord has betaken himself to unknown travels,   35
Now message must return from whence it came.
   Hel. We have no reason to desire it,
Commended to our master, not to us.
Yet, ere you shall depart, this we desire,
As friends to Antioch, we may feast in Tyre.   40
                            Exeunt.

[I.iv.] Cleon, Governor of Tarsus, and his wife, Dionyza, lament the disastrous famine that has brought misery to their city. When a fleet is sighted, they fear that an enemy has come to take advantage of their weakness. The ships, however, are those of Pericles, who seeks a haven in exchange for grain that he has brought to relieve Tarsus. His bounty is received with gratitude.

5. **who:** whoever; **digs:** digs up; **aspire;** tower.

8. **Here they are but felt and seen with mischief's eyes:** as things are, our griefs are precisely known in accordance with the distress they cause us.

9. **like to groves, being topped, they higher rise:** i.e., just as trees are pruned to make them more luxurious, attempts to depreciate our troubles will only make them loom larger.

11. **wanteth:** lacketh.

15. **fetch:** acquire.

17. **That:** so that.

[Scene IV. Tarsus. A room in the Governor's house.]

*Enter Cleon, the Governor of Tarsus, with his wife
[Dionyza] and others.*

Cleon. My Dionyza, shall we rest us here
And by relating tales of others' griefs
See if 'twill teach us to forget our own?
Dio. That were to blow at fire in hope to quench it;
For who digs hills because they do aspire 5
Throws down one mountain to cast up a higher.
O my distressed lord, even such our griefs are!
Here they are but felt and seen with mischief's eyes,
But, like to groves, being topped, they higher rise.
Cleon. O Dionyza, 10
Who wanteth food and will not say he wants it,
Or can conceal his hunger till he famish?
Our tongues and sorrows do sound deep
Our woes into the air; our eyes do weep,
Till tongues fetch breath that may proclaim them 15
louder;
That, if Heaven slumber while their creatures want,
They may awake their helps to comfort them.
I'll then discourse our woes, felt several years,
And wanting breath to speak help me with tears. 20
Dio. I'll do my best, sir.
Cleon. This Tarsus, o'er which I have the govern-
ment,
A city on whom plenty held full hand,
For riches strewed herself even in the streets; 25

29. **jetted:** strutted.
30. **trim:** decorate.
32. **not so much to feed on as delight:** i.e., the dishes set out were more than hunger required, being designed to delight the eye.
46. **nuzzle up:** coddle.
47. **curious:** dainty.

Whose towers bore heads so high they kissed the
    clouds,
And strangers ne'er beheld but wondered at;
Whose men and dames so jetted and adorned,
Like one another's glass to trim them by: **30**
Their tables were stored full, to glad the sight,
And not so much to feed on as delight;
All poverty was scorned and pride so great,
The name of help grew odious to repeat.

  Dio. Oh, 'tis too true.   **35**

  Cleon. But see what Heaven can do! By this our
    change,
These mouths, who but of late earth, sea, and air
Were all too little to content and please,
Although they gave their creatures in abundance,   **40**
As houses are defiled for want of use,
They are now starved for want of exercise.
Those palates who, not yet two summers younger,
Must have inventions to delight the taste
Would now be glad of bread, and beg for it.   **45**
Those mothers who, to nuzzle up their babes,
Thought naught too curious are ready now
To eat those little darlings whom they loved.
So sharp are hunger's teeth that man and wife
Draw lots who first shall die to lengthen life.   **50**
Here stands a lord and there a lady weeping;
Here many sink, yet those which see them fall
Have scarce strength left to give them burial.
Is not this true?

  Dio. Our cheeks and hollow eyes do witness it. **55**

  Cleon. O, let those cities that of plenty's cup

58. **superfluous riots:** extravagant revels.

66. **portly sail:** stately fleet.

68. **One sorrow never comes but brings an heir:** proverbial.

75. **Whereas no glory's got to overcome:** where a conquest can gain no glory.

79. **repeat:** recite (the proverbial idea that follows).

And her prosperities so largely taste,
With their superfluous riots, hear these tears!
The misery of Tarsus may be theirs.

Enter a Lord.

Lord. Where's the Lord Governor?   60
Cleon. Here.
Speak out thy sorrows which thou bringst in haste,
For comfort is too far for us to expect.
Lord. We have descried, upon our neighboring
        shore,   65
A portly sail of ships make hitherward.
Cleon. I thought as much.
One sorrow never comes but brings an heir
That may succeed as his inheritor:
And so in ours, some neighboring nation,   70
Taking advantage of our misery,
Hath stuffed the hollow vessels with their power,
To beat us down the which are down already,
And make a conquest of unhappy me,
Whereas no glory's got to overcome.   75
Lord. That's the least fear; for, by the semblance
Of their white flags displayed, they bring us peace
And come to us as favorers, not as foes.
Cleon. Thou speakst like him 's untutored to repeat:
Who makes the fairest show means most deceit.   80
But bring they what they will and what they can,
What need we fear?
The ground's the lowest, and we are halfway there.

86. **craves:** wishes.

88. **on peace consist:** stand on peaceful terms.

97. **happily:** perhaps.

99. **bloody veins expecting overthrow:** a strange metaphor, which apparently means bloodthirsty soldiers awaiting the chance to overthrow Troy.

100. **corn:** wheat or other grain.

107. **gratify:** satisfy.

108. **pay you:** i.e., if they shall pay you.

Go tell their general we attend him here,
To know for what he comes and whence he comes   85
And what he craves.
    Lord. I go, my lord.   [*Exit.*]
    Cleon. Welcome is peace, if he on peace consist;
If wars, we are unable to resist.

       Enter Pericles with Attendants.

    Per. Lord Governor, for so we hear you are,   90
Let not our ships and number of our men
Be like a beacon fired t' amaze your eyes.
We have heard your miseries as far as Tyre
And seen the desolation of your streets.
Nor come we to add sorrow to your tears,   95
But to relieve them of their heavy load;
And these our ships, you happily may think
Are like the Trojan horse was stuffed within
With bloody veins expecting overthrow,
Are stored with corn to make your needy bread   100
And give them life whom hunger starved half dead.
    Omnes. The gods of Greece protect you!
And we'll pray for you.
    Per.   Arise, I pray you, rise.
We do not look for reverence but for love   105
And harborage for ourself, our ships and men.
    Cleon. The which when any shall not gratify,
Or pay you with unthankfulness in thought,
Be it our wives, our children, or ourselves,

110. succeed: follow upon.

To tell their general state,
To know for what he comes and whence he comes   84
And what he craves.

Lord, I go, my lord.   [Exit]

Cleon. Which welcome we'll accept; if he on peace consist,
If wars, we are unable to resist.

Enter Pericles with Attendants.

Per. Lord Governor, for so we hear you are,   90
Let not our ships and number of our men
Be like a beacon fired t' amaze your eyes.
We have heard your miseries as far as Tyre,
And seen the desolation of your streets;
Nor come we to add sorrow to your tears,   96
But to relieve them of their heavy load;
And these our ships, you happily may think
Are like the Trojan horse was stuffed within
With bloody veins, expecting overthrow,
Are stored with corn to make your needy bread   102
And give them life whom hunger starved half dead.

Omnes. The gods of Greece protect you!
And we'll pray for you.

Per.   Arise, I pray you, rise.
We do not look for reverence but for love,   108
And harbourage for ourself, our ships and men.

Cleon. The which when any shall not gratify,
Or pay you with unthankfulness in thought,
Be it our wives, our children, or ourselves,

The curse of Heaven and men succeed their evils! 110
Till when—the which I hope shall ne'er be seen—
Your Grace is welcome to our town and us.

 Per. Which welcome we'll accept; feast here awhile,
Until our stars that frown lend us a smile.

        Exeunt.

PERICLES
PRINCE OF TYRE

⚜

ACT II

[II.Pro.] Gower describes Pericles' honor in Tarsus, which has erected a statue to commemorate his charity. Gower explains a dumb show that depicts Pericles receiving word from Tyre of Thaliard's visit, with the warning that Tarsus is no longer safe for him. Accordingly, Pericles again sets sail and encounters a fierce tempest.

───

2. **iwis:** indeed (with force "incredible as it may seem").

4. **awful:** worthy of respect.

7. **those:** i.e., those who reign beset by troubles.

9. **conversation:** personal conduct.

10. **benison:** blessing.

11-2. **where each man/ Thinks all is Writ he speken can:** where each citizen thinks every word he utters is Holy Writ.

13. **remember:** commemorate.

14. **glorious:** renowned.

15. **tidings to the contrary:** news calculated to alter this state of affairs.

[*ACT II*]

Enter Gower [as Prologue].

Here have you seen a mighty king
His child, iwis, to incest bring:
A better prince and benign lord,
That will prove awful both in deed and word.
Be quiet then as men should be,   5
Till he hath passed necessity.
I'll show you those in troubles reign,
Losing a mite, a mountain gain.
The good in conversation,
To whom I give my benison,   10
Is still at Tarsus, where each man
Thinks all is Writ he speken can;
And, to remember what he does,
Build his statue to make him glorious.
But tidings to the contrary   15
Are brought your eyes. What need speak I?

Dumb Show.
Enter, at one door, Pericles, talking with Cleon; all the train with them. Enter, at another door, a Gentleman with a letter to Pericles. Pericles shows the letter

21

23. **full bent with:** fully intent upon.
28. **been:** are; an old form like **killen, escapen,** and **speken.**
36. **Ne aught:** naught.
40. **'longs:** belongs to.

to Cleon. Pericles gives the Messenger a reward and
knights him. Exit Pericles at one door and Cleon at
another.

Good Helicane, that stayed at home,
Not to eat honey like a drone
From others' labors; for though he strive
To killen bad, keep good alive;   20
And to fulfill his Prince' desire,
Sends word of all that haps in Tyre:
How Thaliard came full bent with sin
And had intent to murder him;
And that in Tarsus was not best   25
Longer for him to make his rest.
He, doing so, put forth to seas,
Where, when men been, there's seldom ease;
For now the wind begins to blow;
Thunder above and deeps below   30
Makes such unquiet that the ship
Should house him safe is wracked and split;
And he, good Prince, having all lost,
By waves from coast to coast is tost.
All perishen of man, of pelf,   35
Ne aught escapen but himself;
Till fortune, tired with doing bad,
Threw him ashore, to give him glad.
And here he comes. What shall be next,
Pardon old Gower: this 'longs the text.   40

                                        [*Exit.*]

[II.i.] His ship wrecked, Pericles reaches shore near Pentapolis. Three fishermen offer him shelter. When a rusty suit of armor is brought up in a fisherman's net, Pericles recognizes it as one that had belonged to his father. The fishermen agree to let him have it so that he can compete in a tournament in honor of the daughter of Simonides, King of Pentapolis.

━━━━━━━━━━━━━━━━━━━━━━━━

11. **crave:** ask as a favor.
12. **Pilch:** literally, an outer garment made of leather or rough fabric.
17. **wanion:** vengeance.

[Scene I. Pentapolis. An open place by the seaside.]

Enter Pericles, wet.

Per. Yet cease your ire, you angry stars of heaven!
Wind, rain, and thunder, remember earthly man
Is but a substance that must yield to you;
And I, as fits my nature, do obey you.
Alas, the seas hath cast me on the rocks, 5
Washed me from shore to shore, and left my breath
Nothing to think on but ensuing death.
Let it suffice the greatness of your powers
To have bereft a prince of all his fortunes;
And, having thrown him from your wat'ry grave, 10
Here to have death in peace is all he'll crave.

Enter three Fishermen.

1. Fish. What ho, Pilch!
2. Fish. Ha, come and bring away the nets!
1. Fish. What, Patchbreech, I say!
3. Fish. What say you, master? 15
1. Fish. Look how thou stirrst now! Come away, or
I'll fetch thee with a wanion.
3. Fish. Faith, master, I am thinking of the poor
men that were cast away before us even now.
1. Fish. Alas, poor souls, it grieved my heart to 20
hear
What pitiful cries they made to us to help them,
When, well a day, we could scarce help ourselves.

25. porpoise: a portent of stormy weather.

31. 'a: he.

33-4. whales . . . o' the land: possibly referring to the greedy landlords who enclosed land for additional sheep pastures and sometimes depopulated whole villages as a result.

54-6. Honest! . . . after it: the fisherman's reply does not clearly relate to Pericles' greeting. A phrase or sentence referring to the day may have dropped out of Pericles' speech.

The great fish eat up the little ones.
From Geoffrey Whitney, *A Choice of Emblems* (1586).

3. Fish. Nay, master, said not I as much when I saw
the porpoise how he bounced and tumbled? They say 25
they're half fish, half flesh. A plague on them, they
ne'er come but I look to be washed! Master, I marvel
how the fishes live in the sea.

1. Fish. Why, as men do a-land: the great ones eat
up the little ones. I can compare our rich misers to 30
nothing so fitly as to a whale: 'a plays and tumbles,
driving the poor fry before him, and at last devours
them all at a mouthful. Such whales have I heard on
o' the land, who never leave gaping till they swallowed the whole parish, church, steeple, bells, and all. 35

Per. [*Aside*] A pretty moral.

3. Fish. But, master, if I had been the sexton, I
would have been that day in the belfry.

2. Fish. Why, man?

3. Fish. Because he should have swallowed me too; 40
and when I had been in his belly, I would have kept
such a jangling of the bells, that he should never have
left till he cast bells, steeple, church, and parish up
again. But if the good King Simonides were of my
mind— 45

Per. [*Aside*] Simonides!

3. Fish. We would purge the land of these drones,
that rob the bee of her honey.

Per. [*Aside*] How from the finny subject of the sea
These fishers tell the infirmities of men; 50
And from their wat'ry empire recollect
All that may men approve or men detect!—
Peace be at your labor, honest fishermen.

2. Fish. Honest! good fellow, what's that? If it be a

57. May see: "you" is presumably understood.

65. our country of Greece: the best-known historical Pentapolis was in Cyrenaica on the northern coast of Africa. The author probably did not concern himself about precise geographical location.

70. fish: i.e., contrive.

73. thronged up with: mastered by.

78. quotha: said he; **and:** if.

80. afore me: on my word.

A sailor in a sea gown.
From Pietro Bertelli, *Diversarum nationum habitus* (1594).

day fits you, search out of the calendar, and nobody 55
look after it.

Per. May see the sea hath cast upon your coast.

2. Fish. What a drunken knave was the sea to cast
thee in our way!

Per. A man whom both the waters and the wind, 60
In that vast tennis court, hath made the ball
For them to play upon entreats you pity him.
He asks of you that never used to beg.

1. Fish. No, friend, cannot you beg? Here's them
in our country of Greece gets more with begging than 65
we can do with working.

2. Fish. Canst thou catch any fishes then?

Per. I never practiced it.

2. Fish. Nay, then thou wilt starve, sure; for here's
nothing to be got nowadays unless thou canst fish for't. 70

Per. What I have been I have forgot to know;
But what I am want teaches me to think on:
A man thronged up with cold. My veins are chill
And have no more of life than may suffice
To give my tongue that heat to ask your help; 75
Which if you shall refuse, when I am dead,
For that I am a man, pray you see me buried.

1. Fish. Die quotha? Now gods forbid't! and I have
a gown here: come, put it on. Keep thee warm! Now,
afore me, a handsome fellow! Come, thou shalt go 80
home, and we'll have flesh for holidays, fish for fasting days, and moreo'er puddings and flapjacks, and
thou shalt be welcome.

Per. I thank you, sir.

88. **crave:** request.
93. **beadle:** an official who whipped beggars.
114. **things must be as they may:** proverbial.
114-16. **what a man cannot get, he may lawfully deal for——his wife's soul:** i.e., what he cannot earn, he may barter his wife's soul for.

2. Fish. Hark you, my friend. You said you could 85
not beg.

Per. I did but crave.

2. Fish. But crave! Then I'll turn craver too, and
so I shall 'scape whipping.

Per. Why, are all your beggars whipped then? 90

2. Fish. Oh, not all, my friend, not all. For if all
your beggars were whipped, I would wish no better
office than to be beadle. But, master, I'll go draw up
the net. *[Exit with Third Fisherman.]*

Per. *[Aside]* How well this honest mirth becomes 95
their labor!

1. Fish. Hark you, sir, do you know where ye are?

Per. Not well.

1. Fish. Why, I'll tell you: this is called Pentapolis,
and our king the good Simonides. 100

Per. The good Simonides, do you call him?

1. Fish. Ay, sir; and he deserves so to be called for
his peaceable reign and good government.

Per. He is a happy king, since he gains from his
subjects the name of good by his government. How 105
far is his court distant from this shore?

1. Fish. Marry, sir, half a day's journey: and I'll tell
you, he hath a fair daughter, and tomorrow is her
birthday; and there are princes and knights come
from all parts of the world to joust and tourney for 110
her love.

Per. Were my fortunes equal to my desires, I could
wish to make one there.

1. Fish. O sir, things must be as they may; and what

119. bots: a plague; literally, a disease affecting horses.

128. brace: vambrace; mail for the forearm.

139. For: because; **target:** shield.

a man cannot get, he may lawfully deal for—his wife's 115
soul.

Enter the two [other] Fishermen, drawing up a net.

2. Fish. Help, master, help! Here's a fish hangs in
the net like a poor man's right in the law. 'Twill hard-
ly come out. Ha! bots on't, 'tis come at last, and 'tis
turned to a rusty armor.   120
Per. An armor, friends! I pray you, let me see it.
Thanks, Fortune, yet, that after all thy crosses
Thou givest me somewhat to repair myself!
And though it was mine own, part of my heritage,
Which my dead father did bequeath to me,   125
With this strict charge, even as he left his life,
"Keep it, my Pericles; it hath been a shield
'Twixt me and death,"—and pointed to this brace—
"For that it saved me, keep it. In like necessity
(The which the gods protect thee from!) may defend 130
    thee."
It kept where I kept, I so dearly loved it;
Till the rough seas, that spares not any man,
Took it in rage, though calmed have given't again.
I thank thee for't. My shipwrack now's no ill,   135
Since I have here my father gave in his will.
1. Fish. What mean you, sir?
Per. To beg of you, kind friends, this coat of worth,
For it was sometime target to a king.
I know it by this mark. He loved me dearly,   140
And for his sake I wish the having of it;
And that you'd guide me to your sovereign's court,

147. virtue: power.

151. made up this garment: (1) fetched up this garment; (2) put this garment together.

152. condolements: apparently meaning something like vails, i.e., tips, rewards.

157. rapture: violent plunder.

158. holds his building: keeps its place.

159. Unto thy value: i.e., to the amount that can be gained by sale of the jewel.

163. a pair of bases: a separate, pleated skirt that was attached to the bottom of the body armor.

Tournament array.
From Conrad Lycosthenes, *Prodigiorum liber* (1557).

Where with it I may appear a gentleman;
And if that ever my low fortune's better,
I'll pay your bounties; till then rest your debtor.   145

  1. Fish. Why, wilt thou tourney for the lady?
  Per. I'll show the virtue I have borne in arms.
  1. Fish. Why, do 'ee take it, and the gods give thee
good on't!
  2. Fish. Ay, but hark you, my friend; 'twas we that 150
made up this garment through the rough seams of the
waters. There are certain condolements, certain vails.
I hope, sir, if you thrive, you'll remember from
whence you had them.
  Per. Believe't I will.   155
By your furtherance I am clothed in steel;
And, spite of all the rapture of the sea,
This jewel holds his building on my arm.
Unto thy value I will mount myself
Upon a courser whose delightful steps   160
Shall make the gazer joy to see him tread.
Only, my friend, I yet am unprovided
Of a pair of bases.
  2. Fish. We'll sure provide. Thou shalt have my
best gown to make thee a pair; and I'll bring thee to 165
the court myself.
  Per. Then honor be but a goal to my will,
This day I'll rise, or else add ill to ill.

                                        [Exeunt.]

[II.ii.] Simonides' daughter, Thaisa, presides at the tournament. Pericles' mean equipment causes wonder, but Simonides cautions against judging a man by his appearance.

━━━━━━━━━━━━━━━━

1. **triumph:** spectacle.
3. **stay:** await.
4. **Return them:** reply to them.
15. **entertain:** receive graciously.
19. **prefer:** offer.

Plus par doulceur, que par force.

Plus par doulceur, que par force,
a French version of the Second Knight's motto, ll. 29-30.
Here the gentle coercion of the sun is contrasted with the
wind's force. From Giles Corrozet, *Hecatomgraphie* (1543).

[Scene II. Pentapolis. A public way or platform leading to the lists. A pavilion by the side of it for the reception of the King, Princess, Lords, etc.]

Enter Simonides, with Thaisa, [Lords], and Attendants.

Sim. Are the knights ready to begin the triumph?
1. Lord. They are, my liege,
And stay your coming to present themselves.
Sim. Return them we are ready; and our daughter here,   5
In honor of whose birth these triumphs are,
Sits here, like beauty's child, whom nature gat
For men to see and seeing wonder at. *[Exit a Lord.]*
Thaisa. It pleaseth you, my royal father, to express
My commendations great, whose merit's less.   10
Sim. It's fit it should be so; for princes are
A model which Heaven makes like to itself.
As jewels lose their glory if neglected,
So princes their renowns if not respected.
'Tis now your honor, daughter, to entertain   15
The labor of each knight in his device.
Thaisa. Which, to preserve mine honor, I'll perform.

[Enter a Knight; he passes over, and his Squire shows his shield to the Princess.]

Sim. Who is the first that doth prefer himself?
Thaisa. A knight of Sparta, my renowned father;   20

23. word: motto; **Lux tua vita mihi:** your light is my life.

29-30. Piu por dulzura que por fuerza: more by sweetness than by force.

34. Me pompae provexit apex: the crown of glorious achievement prompted me.

37. Qui me alit, me extinguit: who nourishes me, extinguishes me.

38. his: its.

43. Sic spectanda fides: thus fidelity is proved.

The device of the Fourth Knight.
From Geoffrey Whitney, *A Choice of Emblems* (1586).

And the device he bears upon his shield
Is a black Ethiope reaching at the sun;
The word, *Lux tua vita mihi.*
   Sim. He loves you well that holds his life of you.
                The Second Knight [*passes*].
Who is the second that presents himself?   25
   Thaisa. A prince of Macedon, my royal father;
And the device he bears upon his shield
Is an armed knight that's conquered by a lady;
The motto thus, in Spanish, *Piu por dulzura que por
   fuerza.*   *The Third Knight* [*passes*]. 30
   Sim. And what's the third?
   Thaisa.   The third of Antioch;
And his device, a wreath of chivalry;
The word, *Me pompae provexit apex.*
                The Fourth Knight [*passes*].
   Sim. What is the fourth?   35
   Thaisa. A burning torch that's turned upside down;
The word, *Qui me alit, me extinguit.*
   Sim. Which shows that beauty hath his power and
    will,
Which can as well inflame as it can kill.   40
                The Fifth Knight [*passes*].
   Thaisa. The fifth, an hand environed with clouds,
Holding out gold that's by the touchstone tried;
The motto thus, *Sic spectanda fides.*
        The Sixth Knight, [*Pericles, passes*].
   Sim. And what's
The sixth and last, the which the knight himself 45
With such a graceful courtesy delivered?

47. **stranger:** foreigner; **present:** offering.

49. **In hac spe vivo:** in this hope I live.

55. **just commend:** true commendation.

57. **whipstock:** probably for "whipstaff," the handle of a ship's tiller.

62. **Opinion:** conjecture; **scan:** read.

63. **The outward habit by the inward man:** i.e., the outer dress as depicting the inner man.

SD 66. **mean:** meanly dressed.

‖‖

[II.iii.] Pericles is crowned by Thaisa as victor of the tournament, and Simonides gives him a place of honor by his side. Both Simonides and his daughter are greatly impressed by the stranger knight. In answer to their questions, Pericles reveals that he is a gentleman of Tyre, Pericles by name, who was shipwrecked on the shores of Pentapolis. When the knights and ladies of the company dance, Simonides acclaims Pericles as the best of the gentlemen. Bidding the company good night, Simonides postpones until the next day consideration of suits for Thaisa's hand.

The device of the Fifth Knight.
From Geoffrey Whitney, *A Choice of Emblems* (1586).

31

Thaisa. He seems to be a stranger; but his present is
A withered branch that's only green at top;
The motto, *In hac spe vivo.*

   Sim. A pretty moral;   50
From the dejected state wherein he is
He hopes by you his fortunes yet may flourish.

   1. Lord. He had need mean better than his outward
      show
Can any way speak in his just commend;   55
For by his rusty outside he appears
To have practiced more the whipstock than the lance.

   2. Lord. He well may be a stranger, for he comes
To an honored triumph strangely furnished.

   3. Lord. And on set purpose let his armor rust   60
Until this day, to scour it in the dust.

   Sim. Opinion's but a fool, that makes us scan
The outward habit by the inward man.
But stay, the knights are coming: we will withdraw
Into the gallery.   [*Exeunt.*]   65
Great shouts [*within,*] *and all cry,* "The mean knight!"

[Scene III. Pentapolis. A hall of state, a banquet
prepared.]

Enter the King, [*Thaisa, Ladies, Marshal, Lords,*]
Knights from tilting, [*and Attendants*].

   Sim. Knights,
To say you're welcome were superfluous.

6. in show: by demonstration.

17. her labored scholar: the student to whom Art devoted her best labors.

32. cates: delicacies; **resist:** repel; **he but thought upon:** because he fills my thoughts.

A tournament.
From *Le troisième livre d'Amadis de Gaule* (1550).

To place upon the volume of your deeds,
As in a title page, your worth in arms
Were more than you expect, or more than's fit,   5
Since every worth in show commends itself.
Prepare for mirth, for mirth becomes a feast.
You are princes and my guests.

 Thaisa. But you, my knight and guest;
To whom this wreath of victory I give,   10
And crown you king of this day's happiness.

 Per. 'Tis more by fortune, lady, than my merit.

 Sim. Call it by what you will, the day is yours;
And here, I hope, is none that envies it.
In framing an artist, Art hath thus decreed,   15
To make some good, but other to exceed;
And you are her labored scholar. Come, queen o' the
  feast—
For, daughter, so you are—here take your place.—
Marshal, the rest as they deserve their grace.   20

 Knights. We are honored much by good Simonides.

 Sim. Your presence glads our days. Honor we love;
For who hates honor, hates the gods above.

 Mar. Sir, yonder is your place.

 Per.   Some other is more fit.   25

 1. Kni. Contend not, sir; for we are gentlemen
Have neither in our hearts nor outward eyes
Envied the great nor shall the low despise.

 Per. You are right courteous knights.

 Sim.   Sit, sir, sit.   30
[*Aside*] By Jove, I wonder, that is king of thoughts,
These cates resist me, he but thought upon.

 Thaisa. [*Aside*] By Juno, that is queen of marriage,

39. **to:** compared with.
47. **vail:** bow; humble.
62. **show:** spectacle.

All viands that I eat do seem unsavory,
Wishing him my meat. Sure he's a gallant gentleman. 35
   Sim. [*Aside*] He's but a country gentleman;
Has done no more than other knights have done;
Has broken a staff or so: so let it pass.
   Thaisa. [*Aside*] To me he seems like diamond to
     glass. 40
   Per. [*Aside*] Yon king's to me like to my father's
     picture,
Which tells me in that glory once he was;
Had princes sit, like stars, about his throne,
And he the sun, for them to reverence; 45
None that beheld him but, like lesser lights,
Did vail their crowns to his supremacy:
Where now his son's like a glowworm in the night,
The which hath fire in darkness, none in light.
Whereby I see that Time's the king of men: 50
He's both their parent and he is their grave,
And gives them what he will, not what they crave.
   Sim. What, are you merry, knights?
   Knights. Who can be other in this royal presence?
   Sim. Here, with a cup that's stored unto the brim— 55
As do you love, fill to your mistress' lips—
We drink this health to you.
   Knights.   We thank your Grace.
   Sim. Yet pause awhile.
Yon knight doth sit too melancholy, 60
As if the entertainment in our court
Had not a show might countervail his worth.
Note it not you, Thaisa?
   Thaisa. What is't to me, my father?

70. Which make a sound, but killed are wondered at: i.e., who threaten when alive but no longer command any respect when their insignificant power to injure is ended by death.

72. standing bowl: a bowl with a stem or footed base.

78. move: anger.

87-8. pledge him freely: drink his health without reservation.

Sim. O, attend, my daughter.   65
Princes, in this, should live like gods above,
Who freely give to everyone that comes
To honor them:
And princes not doing so are like to gnats,
Which make a sound, but killed are wondered at.   70
Therefore to make his entrance more sweet,
Here say we drink this standing bowl of wine to him.
   Thaisa. Alas, my father, it befits not me
Unto a stranger knight to be so bold.
He may my proffer take for an offense,   75
Since men take women's gifts for impudence.
   Sim. How!
Do as I bid you, or you'll move me else.
   Thaisa. [*Aside*] Now, by the gods, he could not
     please me better.   80
   Sim. And furthermore tell him, we desire to know
     of him,
Of whence he is, his name and parentage.
   Thaisa. The King my father, sir, has drunk to you.
   Per. I thank him.   85
   Thaisa. Wishing it so much blood unto your life.
   Per. I thank both him and you, and pledge him
     freely.
   Thaisa. And further he desires to know of you
Of whence you are, your name and parentage.   90
   Per. A gentleman of Tyre; my name, Pericles;
My education been in arts and arms;
Who, looking for adventures in the world,
Was by the rough seas reft of ships and men,
And after shipwrack driven upon this shore.   95

105. **addressed:** furnished.

111. **breathing:** exercise.

113. **trip:** dance in a lively manner.

114. **measures:** stately dances.

116-17. **that's as much as you would be denied/ Of your fair courtesy:** that's as much as to say that you politely claim no skill yourself.

Thaisa. He thanks your Grace; names himself
    Pericles,
A gentleman of Tyre,
Who only by misfortune of the seas,
Bereft of ships and men, cast on this shore.   100
    Sim. Now, by the gods, I pity his misfortune
And will awake him from his melancholy.
Come, gentlemen, we sit too long on trifles,
And waste the time, which looks for other revels.
Even in your armors, as you are addressed,   105
Will very well become a soldier's dance.
I will not have excuse, with saying this
Loud music is too harsh for ladies' heads,
Since they love men in arms as well as beds.
                              They dance.
So, this was well asked, 'twas so well performed.   110
Come, sir, here's a lady that wants breathing too:
And I have heard you knights of Tyre
Are excellent in making ladies trip,
And that their measures are as excellent.
    Per. In those that practice them they are, my lord. 115
    Sim. Oh, that's as much as you would be denied
Of your fair courtesy.
             [*The Knights and Ladies*] *dance.*
                Unclasp, unclasp!
Thanks, gentlemen, to all. All have done well,
[*To Pericles*] But you the best.—Pages and lights, to 120
    conduct
These knights unto their several lodgings! Yours, sir,
We have given order to be next our own.
    Per. I am at your Grace's pleasure.

128. speeding: success.

━━━━━━━━━━━━━━━━━━━━━━━━━━━━━━━━━

[II.iv.] The lords of Pericles' court are anxious at his continued absence. They announce their desire either to find Pericles alive or determine that he is dead, in which case they will elect Helicanus to rule Tyre. Helicanus persuades them to wait a year before selecting a replacement for Pericles; in the meantime they can seek far and wide for him.

━━━━━━━━━━━━━━━━━━━━━━━━━━━━━━━━━

3. minding: being of a mind.

Sim. Princes, it is too late to talk of love,   125
And that's the mark I know you level at.
Therefore each one betake him to his rest.
Tomorrow all for speeding do their best.

                              [*Exeunt.*]

[Scene IV. Tyre. A room in the Governor's house.]

Enter Helicanus and Escanes.

Hel. No, Escanes, know this of me,
Antiochus from incest lived not free:
For which, the most high gods not minding longer
To withhold the vengeance that they had in store,
Due to this heinous capital offense,   5
Even in the height and pride of all his glory,
When he was seated in a chariot
Of an inestimable value, and his daughter with him,
A fire from heaven came and shriveled up
Their bodies, even to loathing; for they so stunk   10
That all those eyes adored them ere their fall
Scorn now their hand should give them burial.
     Esc. 'Twas very strange.
     Hel.   And yet but justice; for though
This king were great, his greatness was no guard   15
To bar Heaven's shaft, but sin had his reward.
     Esc. 'Tis very true.

          Enter two or three Lords.

20. It shall no longer grieve without reproof: we shall no longer endure this grievance without complaint.

36-7. the strongest in our censure: i.e., seems to our judgment the likeliest possibility.

44. forbear your suffrages: relinquish your right to elect (Helicanus to replace Pericles).

46. Take I: if I take.

1. Lord. See, not a man in private conference
Or council has respect with him but he.

2. Lord. It shall no longer grieve without reproof.   20

3. Lord. And cursed be he that will not second it.

1. Lord. Follow me then. Lord Helicane, a word.

Hel. With me? and welcome. Happy day, my lords.

1. Lord. Know that our griefs are risen to the top,
And now at length they overflow their banks.   25

Hel. Your griefs! For what? Wrong not your prince
     you love.

1. Lord. Wrong not yourself, then, noble Helicane;
But if the Prince do live, let us salute him,
Or know what ground's made happy by his breath.   30
If in the world he live, we'll seek him out;
If in his grave he rest, we'll find him there;
And be resolved he lives to govern us,
Or dead, give 's cause to mourn his funeral
And leave us to our free election.   35

2. Lord. Whose death indeed the strongest in our
     censure:
And knowing this kingdom is without a head—
Like goodly buildings left without a roof
Soon fall to ruin—your noble self,   40
That best know how to rule and how to reign,
We thus submit unto, our sovereign.

Omnes. Live, noble Helicane!

Hel. For honor's cause, forbear your suffrages.
If that you love Prince Pericles, forbear.   45
Take I your wish, I leap into the seas,
Where's hourly trouble for a minute's ease.
A twelvemonth longer let me entreat you

49. forbear: endure.

[II.v.] Thaisa has announced her decision not to marry for a year but to remain a votaress of the goddess Diana for that term. In a private communication to Simonides, the Princess has made known her love for Pericles and her determination to marry no one else. Simonides is well pleased but tests Pericles by showing him the letter. Pericles denies having courted Thaisa, but when she frankly reveals her love, he declares his love for her. Simonides plans an immediate wedding.

To forbear the absence of your king;
If in which time expired he not return,   50
I shall with aged patience bear your yoke.
But if I cannot win you to this love,
Go search like nobles, like noble subjects,
And in your search spend your adventurous worth;
Whom if you find and win unto return,   55
You shall like diamonds sit about his crown.

   1. Lord. To wisdom he's a fool that will not yield;
And since Lord Helicane enjoineth us,
We with our travels will endeavor it.

   Hel. Then you love us, we you, and we'll clasp   60
    hands.
When peers thus knit, a kingdom ever stands.

                            [Exeunt.]

[Scene V. Pentapolis. A room in the palace.]

Enter the King, reading of a letter, at one door; the
Knights meet him.

   1. Kni. Good morrow to the good Simonides.

   Sim. Knights, from my daughter this I let you
    know:
That for this twelvemonth she'll not undertake
A married life.   5
Her reason to herself is only known,
Which from her by no means can I get.

   2. Kni. May we not get access to her, my lord?

11. **Diana's livery:** the white clothing of a virgin dedicated to the service of the goddess Diana.

12. **the eye of Cynthia:** i.e., the moon, **Cynthia** being another name for Diana as moon-goddess.

19. **nor . . . nor:** neither . . . nor.

Diana, the moon-goddess.
From Vincenzo Cartari, *Imagini delli dei de gl'antichi* (1674).

Sim. Faith, by no means; she hath so strictly tied
Her to her chamber that 'tis impossible.   10
One twelve moons more she'll wear Diana's livery:
This by the eye of Cynthia hath she vowed,
And on her virgin honor will not break it.
   3. Kni. Loath to bid farewell, we take our leaves.
                        [Exeunt Knights.]
   Sim. So,   15
They are well dispatched. Now to my daughter's
    letter.
She tells me here she'll wed the stranger knight,
Or never more to view nor day nor light.
'Tis well, mistress: your choice agrees with mine.   20
I like that well: nay, how absolute she's in't,
Not minding whether I dislike or no!
Well, I do commend her choice;
And will no longer have it be delayed.
Soft! here he comes. I must dissemble it.   25

Enter Pericles.

   Per. All fortune to the good Simonides!
   Sim. To you as much, sir! I am beholding to you
For your sweet music this last night. I do
Protest my ears were never better fed
With such delightful pleasing harmony.   30
   Per. It is your Grace's pleasure to commend,
Not my desert.
   Sim.   Sir, you are music's master.
   Per. The worst of all her scholars, my good lord.
   Sim. Let me ask you one thing: 35

44. **else:** i.e., that proves otherwise.
47. **subtilty:** cunning.
51. **bent all offices:** devoted every faculty.
55. **levy offense:** possibly, "muster for offensive action," but editors have conjectured that **levy** may be an error for "level" (aim).
66. **relished:** smacked; tasted.

What do you think of my daughter, sir?

  Per. A most virtuous princess.

  Sim. And she is fair, too, is she not?

  Per. As a fair day in summer, wondrous fair.

  Sim. Sir, my daughter thinks very well of you;   40
Ay, so well, that you must be her master,
And she will be your scholar. Therefore look to it.

  Per. I am unworthy for her schoolmaster.

  Sim. She thinks not so: peruse this writing else.

  Per. [*Aside*] What's here?   45
A letter, that she loves the knight of Tyre!
'Tis the King's subtilty to have my life.—
O, seek not to entrap me, gracious lord,
A stranger and distressed gentleman,
That never aimed so high to love your daughter   50
But bent all offices to honor her.

  Sim. Thou has bewitched my daughter, and thou art
A villain.

  Per.   By the gods, I have not.
Never did thought of mine levy offense;   55
Nor never did my actions yet commence
A deed might gain her love or your displeasure.

  Sim. Traitor, thou liest.

  Per.   Traitor!

  Sim.   Ay, traitor.   60

  Per. Even in his throat—unless it be the King—
That calls me traitor, I return the lie.

  Sim. [*Aside*] Now, by the gods, I do applaud his
    courage.

  Per. My actions are as noble as my thoughts,   65
That never relished of a base descent.

74. **Resolve:** satisfy.
79. **peremptory:** positive.
91. **seal:** confirm.

I came unto your court for honor's cause,
And not to be a rebel to her state;
And he that otherwise accounts of me,
This sword shall prove he's honor's enemy.   70
  Sim. No?
Here comes my daughter, she can witness it.

Enter Thaisa.

  Per. Then, as you are as virtuous as fair,
Resolve your angry father if my tongue
Did e'er solicit or my hand subscribe   75
To any syllable that made love to you.
  Thaisa. Why, sir, say if you had,
Who takes offense at that would make me glad?
  Sim. Yea, mistress, are you so peremptory?
(*Aside*) I am glad on't with all my heart.—   80
I'll tame you; I'll bring you in subjection.
Will you, not having my consent,
Bestow your love and your affections
Upon a stranger?—(*Aside*) who, for aught I know,
May be, nor can I think the contrary,   85
As great in blood as I myself.—
Therefore hear you, mistress: either frame
Your will to mine—and you, sir, hear you,
Either be ruled by me, or I'll make you—
Man and wife.   90
Nay, come, your hands and lips must seal it too.
And being joined, I'll thus your hopes destroy;
And for a further grief—God give you joy!
What, are you both pleased?

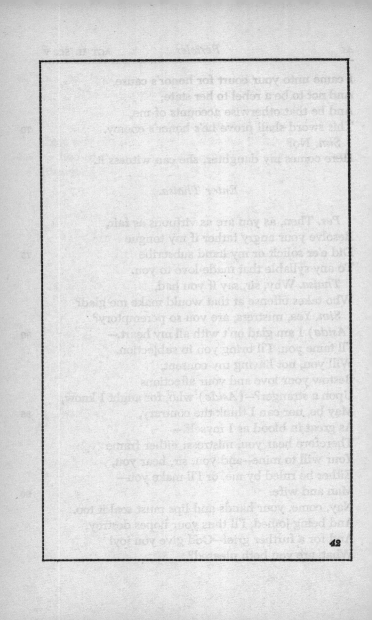

Thaisa.   Yes, if you love me, sir.   95
Per. Even as my life, my blood that fosters it.
Sim. What, are you both agreed?
Ambo. Yes, if't please your Majesty.
    Sim. It pleaseth me so well that I will see you wed;
And then, with what haste you can, get you to bed.   100

                              [*Exeunt.*]

PERICLES
PRINCE OF TYRE

❦

ACT III

[III.Pro.] Gower reports the consummation of the marriage and the conception of a child. A dumb show portrays Pericles' receipt of a letter containing happy news. Gower explains that the letter reports the death of Antiochus and his daughter and that Pericles' lords, thinking Pericles dead, wish to crown Helicanus. Pericles must return to Tyre, and the pregnant Thaisa insists upon accompanying him. A great storm buffets the ship, and in the midst of it Thaisa begins her travail.

1. **yslacked hath:** hath relaxed; **rout:** company.

4. **pompous:** splendid.

5. **eyen:** eyes.

9. **Hymen:** a Greek god regarded as patron of marriage.

11. **attent:** attentive.

13. **quaintly:** ingeniously; **eche:** eke out; supplement.

14. **plain:** make plain.

[*ACT III*]

Enter Gower [as Prologue].

Now sleep yslacked hath the rout:
No din but snores the house about,
Made louder by the o'erfed breast
Of this most pompous marriage feast.
The cat, with eyen of burning coal, 5
Now couches fore the mouse's hole;
And crickets sing at the oven's mouth,
Are the blither for their drouth.
Hymen hath brought the bride to bed,
Where, by the loss of maidenhead, 10
A babe is molded. Be attent,
And time that is so briefly spent
With your fine fancies quaintly eche.
What's dumb in show I'll plain with speech.

[Dumb Show.]

Enter Pericles and Simonides, at one door, with Attendants; a Messenger meets them, kneels, and gives Pericles a letter. Pericles shows it Simonides; the Lords kneel to him. Then enter Thaisa with child,

43

15. **dern:** obscure; difficult; **painful perch:** plot that was difficult to traverse; a **perch** was a measure of land equal to about five and a half yards.

17. **coigns:** corners.

21. **stead:** support.

22. **Fame answering the most strange inquire:** rumor replying to inquiry in the most remote parts.

32. **dooms:** judgments.

36. **can:** 'gan; began.

39. **Brief:** in short.

with Lychorida, a nurse. The King shows her the let-
ter; she rejoices: she and Pericles take leave of her
father and depart [with Lychorida and their Attend-
ants. Then exeunt Simonides and the rest].

By many a dern and painful perch   15
Of Pericles the careful search,
By the four opposing coigns
Which the world together joins,
Is made with all due diligence
That horse and sail and high expense   20
Can stead the quest. At last from Tyre,
Fame answering the most strange inquire,
To the court of King Simonides
Are letters brought, the tenor these:
Antiochus and his daughter dead;   25
The men of Tyrus on the head
Of Helicanus would set on
The crown of Tyre, but he will none.
The mutiny he there hastes t' oppress;
Says to 'em, if King Pericles   30
Come not home in twice six moons,
He, obedient to their dooms,
Will take the crown. The sum of this,
Brought hither to Pentapolis,
Yravished the regions round,   35
And everyone with claps can sound,
"Our heir apparent is a king!
Who dreamt, who thought of such a thing?"
Brief, he must hence depart to Tyre.
His queen with child makes her desire—   40

47. grisled North: grizzled, or hoary, North wind, who as Boreas was usually pictured as an elderly man with grizzled hair and beard, see cut page 46.

51. wellaneer: alas; lamentably.

53. fell: fierce.

55. nill: will not.

56. Conveniently: appropriately.

57. Which might not what by me is told: i.e., action might not so properly convey the events just related.

58. hold: consider.

[III.i.] As Pericles invokes the gods to still the storm, Lychorida, Thaisa's servingwoman and nurse, brings in his newborn daughter and reports that the Queen is dead. The sailors insist that the body must be thrown overboard at once to avert bad luck. Pericles reluctantly bestows the body in a well-caulked casket, along with an identification of Thaisa and a store of jewels. Learning that they are near Tarsus and can reach it by daybreak, he orders the ship's course altered to make for it rather than for Tyre. At Tarsus he can leave the infant in the care of Cleon and Dionyza.

---

1. vast: waste; immense space.

2. thou: addressing Aeolus, god of the winds.

3. bind them in brass: Aeolus is said to have imprisoned the winds in a cave, but his island home is described by classical writers as being surrounded by a metal wall, bronze being specified by Homer.

Which who shall cross?—along to go.
Omit we all their dole and woe.
Lychorida, her nurse, she takes,
And so to sea. Their vessel shakes
On Neptune's billow. Half the flood   45
Hath their keel cut: but Fortune's mood
Varies again; the grisled North
Disgorges such a tempest forth,
That, as a duck for life that dives,
So up and down the poor ship drives.   50
The lady shrieks and wellaneer
Does fall in travail with her fear;
And what ensues in this fell storm
Shall for itself, itself perform.
I nill relate, action may   55
Conveniently the rest convey;
Which might not what by me is told.
In your imagination hold
This stage the ship, upon whose deck
The seatost Pericles appears to speak.   60

           [Exit.]

[Scene I.]

Enter Pericles, a-shipboard.

Per. The god of this great vast, rebuke these surges,
Which wash both Heaven and hell; and thou that hast
Upon the winds command, bind them in brass,

16. **conceit:** understanding.

30. **Even:** if only; **charge:** responsibility (the infant).

Boreas, the "grisled" North wind.
From Gabriele Simeoni, *La vita et Metamorfoseo d'Ovidio* (1559).

Having called them from the deep! O, still
Thy deaf'ning dreadful thunders; gently quench   5
Thy nimble sulphurous flashes!—O, how, Lychorida,
How does my queen?—Thou stormest venomously;
Wilt thou spit all thyself? The seaman's whistle
Is as a whisper in the ears of death,
Unheard.—Lychorida!—Lucina, O   10
Divinest patroness and midwife gentle
To those that cry by night, convey thy deity
Aboard our dancing boat; make swift the pangs
Of my queen's travails!—Now, Lychorida!

Enter Lychorida, [with an Infant].

   Lych. Here is a thing too young for such a place,   15
Who, if it had conceit, would die, as I
Am like to do. Take in your arms this piece
Of your dead queen.
   Per.   How, how, Lychorida!
   Lych. Patience, good sir: do not assist the storm.   20
Here's all that is left living of your queen,
A little daughter. For the sake of it,
Be manly and take comfort.
   Per.   O you gods!
Why do you make us love your goodly gifts   25
And snatch them straight away? We here below
Recall not what we give, and therein may
Vie honor with you.
   Lych.   Patience, good sir,
Even for this charge.   30
   Per.   Now, mild may be thy life!

34. the rudeliest welcome: bid welcome in the roughest manner.

39-40. than can thy portage quit/ With all thou canst find here: i.e., than can be matched by all that you can possibly gain on earth.

43. flaw: storm.

47. bowlines: ropes attached to the middle of the outside of a square sail to hold the sail closer to the wind; **Thou wilt not:** addressed to the storm: "You won't let up."

49. But searoom: if only there is enough room to avoid running the ship aground; **and:** if.

52. lie: subside.

55. still: always.

57. briefly: quickly; **straight:** at once.

58. meet: proper.

Lucina.
From Vincenzo Cartari, *Le imagini de gl' dei de gli antichi* (1609).

For a more blustrous birth had never babe:
Quiet and gentle thy conditions! for
Thou art the rudeliest welcome to this world
That ever was prince's child. Happy what follows!   35
Thou hast as chiding a nativity
As fire, air, water, earth, and heaven can make,
To herald thee from the womb. Even at the first
Thy loss is more than can thy portage quit
With all thou canst find here. Now, the good gods   40
Throw their best eyes upon't!

Enter two Sailors.

1. Sail. What courage, sir? God save you!
Per. Courage enough. I do not fear the flaw:
It hath done to me the worst. Yet, for the love
Of this poor infant, this fresh-new seafarer,   45
I would it would be quiet.
1. Sail. Slack the bowlines there!—Thou wilt not,
wilt thou? Blow, and split thyself.
2. Sail. But searoom, and the brine and cloudy billow kiss the moon, I care not.   50
1. Sail. Sir, your queen must overboard. The sea
works high; the wind is loud and will not lie till the
ship be cleared of the dead.
Per. That's your superstition.
1. Sail. Pardon us, sir: with us at sea it hath been still   55
observed; and we are strong in custom. Therefore
briefly yield 'er; for she must overboard straight.
Per. As you think meet. Most wretched queen!
Lych. Here she lies, sir.

65. **for:** instead of.

66. **aye-remaining lamps:** perpetual lights, such as were placed in burial vaults.

75. **bitumed:** waterproofed with bitumen.

79. **for Tyre:** i.e., the course that is now set for Tyre.

Per. A terrible childbed hast thou had, my dear: 60
No light, no fire. The unfriendly elements
Forgot thee utterly. Nor have I time
To give thee hallowed to thy grave but straight
Must cast thee, scarcely coffined, in the ooze;
Where, for a monument upon thy bones 65
And aye-remaining lamps, the belching whale
And humming water must o'erwhelm thy corpse,
Lying with simple shells. O Lychorida,
Bid Nestor bring me spices, ink, and paper,
My casket and my jewels; and bid Nicander 70
Bring me the satin coffer. Lay the babe
Upon the pillow. Hie thee, whiles I say
A priestly farewell to her. Suddenly, woman!

        [Exit Lychorida.]

2. Sail. Sir, we have a chest beneath the hatches,
Caulked and bitumed ready. 75
 Per. I thank thee. Mariner, say what coast is this?
 2. Sail. We are near Tarsus.
 Per. Thither, gentle mariner,
Alter thy course for Tyre. When canst thou reach it?
 2. Sail. By break of day, if the wind cease. 80
 Per. Oh, make for Tarsus!
There will I visit Cleon, for the babe
Cannot hold out to Tyrus. There I'll leave it
At careful nursing. Go thy ways, good mariner.
I'll bring the body presently. 85

        [Exeunt.]

[III.ii.] The casket of Thaisa is brought to Lord Cerimon of Ephesus, who is deeply learned in medicine. When he views the body he immediately suspects that Thaisa is still alive. She returns to consciousness and is moved to another room, where Cerimon treats her to restore the spark of life.

18. **as:** as though.

[Scene II. Ephesus. A room in Cerimon's house.]

*Enter Lord Cerimon, with a Servant [and some
Persons who have been shipwrecked].*

Cer. Philemon, ho!

Enter Philemon.

Phil. Doth my lord call?
Cer. Get fire and meat for these poor men.
'T has been a turbulent and stormy night.
  Ser. I have been in many; but such a night as this,   **5**
Till now, I ne'er endured.
  Cer. Your master will be dead ere you return.
There's nothing can be ministered to nature
That can recover him. [*To Philemon*] Give this to
  the 'pothecary,   **10**
And tell me how it works. [*Exeunt all but Cerimon.*]

Enter two Gentlemen.

  1. Gent.   Good morrow.
  2. Gent. Good morrow to your Lordship.
  Cer.   Gentlemen,
Why do you stir so early?   **15**
  1. Gent. Sir,
Our lodgings, standing bleak upon the sea,
Shook as the earth did quake.

19. **principals:** principal rafters or other supports.

23. **husbandry:** industry.

26-7. **having/ Rich tire about you:** being surrounded with luxury.

30. **pain:** taking of trouble.

33. **cunning:** learning; skill.

42. **vegetives:** plants.

47. **tottering:** shaky; unreliable.

49. **To please the fool and Death:** i.e., both the fool and Death would ridicule such folly, a metaphor from the illustrations of the Dance of Death.

The very principals did seem to rend
And all to topple. Pure surprise and fear   20
Made me to quit the house.
   2. Gent. That is the cause we trouble you so early:
'Tis not our husbandry.
   Cer.   Oh, you say well.
   1. Gent. But I much marvel that your Lordship,   25
    having
Rich tire about you, should at these early hours
Shake off the golden slumber of repose.
'Tis most strange
Nature should be so conversant with pain,   30
Being thereto not compelled.
   Cer.   I hold it ever,
Virtue and cunning were endowments greater
Than nobleness and riches. Careless heirs
May the two latter darken and expend,   35
But immortality attends the former,
Making a man a god. 'Tis known I ever
Have studied physic, through which secret art,
By turning o'er authorities, I have,
Together with my practice, made familiar   40
To me and to my aid the blest infusions
That dwells in vegetives, in metals, stones;
And I can speak of the disturbances
That Nature works, and of her cures: which doth give
    me   45
A more content in course of true delight
Than to be thirsty after tottering honor,
Or tie my treasure up in silken bags,
To please the fool and Death.

70. close: tightly.

2. *Gent.* Your honor has through Ephesus poured 50
    forth
Your charity, and hundreds call themselves
Your creatures who by you have been restored.
And not your knowledge, your personal pain, but
    even 55
Your purse, still open, hath built Lord Cerimon
Such strong renown as time shall never raze.

    Enter two or three [Servants] with a chest.

    Ser. So: lift there.
    Cer. What's that?
    Ser. Sir, even now 60
Did the sea toss up upon our shore this chest.
'Tis of some wrack.
    Cer.   Set't down, let's look upon't.
    2. *Gent.* 'Tis like a coffin, sir.
    Cer.   Whate'er it be, 65
'Tis wondrous heavy. Wrench it open straight.
If the sea's stomach be o'ercharged with gold,
'Tis a good constraint of fortune it belches upon us.
    2. *Gent.* 'Tis so, my lord.
    Cer. How close 'tis caulked and bitumed! 70
Did the sea cast it up?
    Ser. I never saw so huge a billow, sir,
As tossed it upon shore.
    Cer.   Wrench it open.
Soft! it smells most sweetly in my sense.
    2. *Gent.* A delicate odor. 75
    Cer. As ever hit my nostril. So, up with it.

78. **corse:** corpse.

82. **passport:** certificate of identification.

83. **Apollo:** sometimes considered the patron of learning; **perfect me in the characters:** enable me to understand the writing.

87. **mundane:** worldly.

91. **requite:** reward.

99. **usurp on nature:** unjustly seize one whose time to die has not yet come.

103. **good appliance:** proper medical treatment.

O you most potent gods! What's here? a corse!

  1. Gent. Most strange!

  Cer. Shrouded in cloth of state; balmed and en-   **80**
    treasured

With full bags of spices! A passport too!

Apollo, perfect me in the characters!

         [Reads from a scroll.]

   "Here I give to understand,

     If e'er this coffin drives a-land,   **85**

     I, King Pericles, have lost

     This queen, worth all our mundane cost.

     Who finds her, give her burying:

     She was the daughter of a king.

     Besides this treasure for a fee,   **90**

     The gods requite his charity!"

If thou livest, Pericles, thou hast a heart

That ever cracks for woe! This chanced tonight.

  2. Gent. Most likely, sir.

  Cer.   Nay, certainly tonight;   **95**

For look how fresh she looks! They were too rough

That threw her in the sea. Make a fire within.

Fetch hither all my boxes in my closet.

         [Exit a Servant.]

Death may usurp on nature many hours

And yet the fire of life kindle again   **100**

The o'erpressed spirits. I heard of an Egyptian

That had nine hours lien dead,

Who was by good appliance recovered.

  Enter [a Servant,] with [boxes,] napkins, and fire.

104. **said:** i.e., done.

107. **How thou stirrst, thou block:** addressed to the servant for not moving quickly enough.

121. **water:** luster.

129. **gentle:** courteous.

132. **is mortal:** must be fatal.

133. **Aesculapius:** the Greek god of healing.

Aesculapius.
From Vincenzo Cartari, *Le . . . Imagini de gli dei delli antichi*
(1615).

Well said, well said! The fire and cloths!
The rough and woeful music that we have, 105
Cause it to sound, beseech you.
The viol once more. How thou stirrst, thou block!
The music there! I pray you, give her air.
Gentlemen,
This queen will live: nature awakes; a warmth 110
Breathes out of her. She hath not been entranced
Above five hours. See how she 'gins to blow
Into life's flower again!

    1. Gent.   The Heavens,
Through you, increase our wonder, and sets up 115
Your fame forever.

    Cer.   She is alive: behold,
Her eyelids, cases to those heavenly jewels
Which Pericles hath lost, begin to part
Their fringes of bright gold. The diamonds 120
Of a most praised water doth appear
To make the world twice rich. Live,
And make us weep to hear your fate, fair creature,
Rare as you seem to be.   *She moves.*

    Thaisa.   O dear Diana, 125
Where am I? Where's my lord? What world is this?

    2. Gent. Is not this strange?

    1. Gent. Most rare.

    Cer. Hush, my gentle neighbors!
Lend me your hands: to the next chamber bear her. 130
Get linen. Now this matter must be looked to,
For her relapse is mortal. Come, come!
And Aesculapius guide us!

                They carry her away. Exeunt omnes.

[III.iii.] Pericles leaves his infant daughter, Marina, in the care of Lychorida, Cleon, and Dionyza. The rulers of Tarsus promise to repay Pericles' kindness by their care of his child, while he returns to Tyre.

━━━━━━━━━━━━━━━━━━

3. litigious: quarrelsome.

5. Make up the rest upon you: make up for my deficiency in rewarding you as you deserve.

17. For: because.

18. charge: burden.

24. still: ever.

25. on: of.

[Scene III. Tarsus. A room in the Governor's house.]

Enter Pericles, Cleon, Dionyza, [and Lychorida,
with Marina in her arms].

   Per. Most honored Cleon, I must needs be gone:
My twelve months are expired, and Tyrus stands
In a litigious peace. You, and your lady,
Take from my heart all thankfulness! The gods
Make up the rest upon you!   5
   Cleon. Your shakes of fortune, though they hurt
     you mortally,
Yet glance full woundingly on us.
   Dio.   Oh, your sweet queen!
That the strict Fates had pleased you had brought 10
     her hither,
To have blessed mine eyes with her!
   Per.   We cannot but obey
The powers above us. Could I rage and roar
As doth the sea she lies in, yet the end   15
Must be as 'tis. My gentle babe Marina, whom,
For she was born at sea, I have named so, here
I charge your charity withal, leaving her
The infant of your care; beseeching you
To give her princely training, that she may be   20
Mannered as she is born.
   Cleon.   Fear not, my lord, but think
Your Grace, that fed my country with your corn,
For which the people's prayers still fall upon you,
Must in your child be thought on. If neglection   25

26. **common body:** populace.

30. **To the end of generation:** until my family line is extinct.

40. **to my respect:** in my regard.

45. **masked:** momentarily concealing the hostility that he has previously shown.

50. **grace:** favor.

Neptune, god of the sea.
From Andrea Alciati, *Emblemata* (1577).

Should therein make me vile, the common body,
By you relieved, would force me to my duty.
But if to that my nature need a spur,
The gods revenge it upon me and mine,
To the end of generation!   30
  Per.   I believe you:
Your honor and your goodness teach me to't
Without your vows. Till she be married, madam,
By bright Diana, whom we honor, all
Unscissored shall this hair of mine remain,   35
Though I show ill in't. So I take my leave.
Good madam, make me blessed in your care
In bringing up my child.
  Dio.   I have one myself,
Who shall not be more dear to my respect
Than yours, my lord.   40
  Per.   Madam, my thanks and prayers.
  Cleon. We'll bring your Grace e'en to the edge o'
    the shore,
Then give you up to the masked Neptune and   45
The gentlest winds of Heaven.
  Per.   I will embrace
Your offer. Come, dearest madam. O, no tears,
Lychorida, no tears.
Look to your little mistress, on whose grace   50
You may depend hereafter. Come, my lord.
                                              [*Exeunt.*]

[III.iv.] Cerimon gives Thaisa the articles found in her coffin. She remembers the voyage but does not recall whether her child was born at sea. Fearing that she will never again see Pericles, she decides to become a votaress of Diana's temple at Ephesus.

---

3. **character:** handwriting.
6. **eaning time:** time of childbirth.
10. **take me to:** have recourse to.
14. **date:** term of life.

[Scene IV. Ephesus. A room in Cerimon's house.]

Enter Cerimon and Thaisa.

Cer. Madam, this letter and some certain jewels
Lay with you in your coffer, which are
At your command. Know you the character?
   Thaisa. It is my lord's.
That I was shipped at sea, I well remember,   5
Even on my eaning time; but whether there
Delivered, by the holy gods,
I cannot rightly say. But since King Pericles,
My wedded lord, I ne'er shall see again,
A vestal livery will I take me to   10
And nevermore have joy.
   Cer. Madam, if this you purpose as ye speak,
Diana's temple is not distant far,
Where you may abide till your date expire.
Moreover, if you please, a niece of mine   15
Shall there attend you.
   Thaisa. My recompense is thanks, that's all;
Yet my good will is great, though the gift small.
                            Exeunt.

PERICLES

PRINCE OF TYRE

ACT IV

[IV.Pro.] Gower tells how Marina has blossomed and become the wonder of Tarsus; she has thus incurred the jealousy of Dionyza, whose own daughter Marina eclipses. Deciding that Marina must be put out of the way, Dionyza calls in Leonine to commission her murder.

⁣

6. **fast-growing:** rapidly changing.
10. **heart and place:** central focus.
15. **kind:** manner.
17. **Even:** exactly.
18. **Hight:** is called.
21. **sleided:** made into filaments for weaving.

[ACT IV]

Enter Gower [as Prologue].

Imagine Pericles arrived at Tyre,
Welcomed and settled to his own desire.
His woeful queen we leave at Ephesus,
Unto Diana there's a votaress.
Now to Marina bend your mind,   5
Whom our fast-growing scene must find
At Tarsus and by Cleon trained
In music, letters; who hath gained
Of education all the grace,
Which makes her both the heart and place   10
Of general wonder. But, alack,
That monster envy, oft the wrack
Of earned praise, Marina's life
Seeks to take off by treason's knife.
And in this kind: our Cleon hath   15
One daughter, and a full-grown wench,
Even ripe for marriage rite. This maid
Hight Philoten; and it is said
For certain in our story she
Would ever with Marina be.   20
Be't when she weaved the sleided silk
With fingers long, small, white as milk;

26. **night bird:** nightingale.

27. **still records with moan:** ever warbles mournfully (with reference to the mythological tale of Philomela's transformation to a nightingale, in which form she bemoaned her rape and mutilation).

28. **rich:** cultivated; **constant:** devoted.

29. **Vail:** pay homage to.

31. **absolute:** perfect.

32. **dove of Paphos:** i.e., one of Venus' doves. Paphos, a city on the isle of Cyprus, was one of the centers where Venus was worshiped.

34-5. **as debts,/ And not as given:** i.e., humbly, not in a patronizing manner.

36. **graceful marks:** signs of grace.

38. **present:** immediate.

41. **stead:** assist.

44. **pregnant:** receptive.

45. **Prest:** ready.

48. **Post:** speedily, as though by post horse.

Or when she would with sharp needle wound
The cambric, which she made more sound
By hurting it; or when to the lute   25
She sung and made the night bird mute
That still records with moan; or when
She would with rich and constant pen
Vail to her mistress Dian; still
This Philoten contends in skill   30
With absolute Marina. So
With dove of Paphos might the crow
Vie feathers white. Marina gets
All praises, which are paid as debts,
And not as given. This so darks   35
In Philoten all graceful marks,
That Cleon's wife, with envy rare,
A present murderer does prepare
For good Marina, that her daughter
Might stand peerless by this slaughter.   40
The sooner her vile thoughts to stead,
Lychorida, our nurse, is dead:
And cursed Dionyza hath
The pregnant instrument of wrath
Prest for this blow. The unborn event   45
I do commend to your content:
Only I carry winged Time
Post on the lame feet of my rhyme;
Which never could I so convey
Unless your thoughts went on my way.   50
Dionyza does appear,
With Leonine, a murderer.

                                          Exit.

[IV.i.] Leonine is reluctant, but Dionyza persuades him to kill Marina. The girl appears, with flowers for the grave of Lychorida, who has recently died. Dionyza suggests that it would cheer her to take a walk along the seashore with Leonine. A company of pirates, who seize Marina and carry her off, thwart Leonine's plan to kill the girl.

▬▬▬▬▬▬▬▬▬▬▬▬

6. nicely: as applied to conscience the sense would be "overscrupulously," but with flaming love the sense "wantonly" would be more appropriate. Since the passage is probably corrupt, the precise intent is impossible to determine.

14. Tellus: one of the names for the personification of the earth; **weed:** garment (the flowers which clothe her).

Tellus, the earth goddess.
From Vincenzo Cartari, *Le imagini de gl' dei de gli antichi* (1609).

[Scene I. Tarsus. An open place near the seashore.]

Enter Dionyza, with Leonine.

Dio. Thy oath remember: thou hast sworn to do't.
'Tis but a blow which never shall be known.
Thou canst not do a thing in the world so soon
To yield thee so much profit. Let not conscience,
Which is but cold, or flaming love thy bosom   5
Enslave too nicely; nor let pity, which
Even women have cast off, melt thee, but be
A soldier to thy purpose.

   Leon. I will do't; but yet she is a goodly creature.

   Dio. The fitter then the gods should have her.   10
Here she comes weeping for her only mistress' death.
Thou art resolved?

   Leon. I am resolved.

Enter Marina, with a basket of flowers.

   Mar. No, I will rob Tellus of her weed,
To strew thy green with flowers: the yellows, blues,   15
The purple violets, and marigolds
Shall, as a carpet, hang upon thy grave,
While summer days do last. Ay me! poor maid,
Born in a tempest when my mother died,
This world to me is like a lasting storm,   20
Whirring me from my friends.

   Dio. How now, Marina! Why do you keep alone?
How chance my daughter is not with you? Do not

24. Consume your blood with sorrowing: referring to the belief that sighing drained blood from the heart.

25. of: in; **favor:** beauty.

27. margent: edge.

28. quick: sharp.

29. stomach: appetite.

35. foreign: distant, as though a stranger.

37. to: by.

41. reserve: save.

Consume your blood with sorrowing: you have
A nurse of me. Lord, how your favor's changed   25
With this unprofitable woe! Come,
Give me your flowers. Near the sea margent
Walk with Leonine: the air is quick there
And it pierces and sharpens the stomach. Come,
Leonine, take her by the arm, walk with her.   30
 Mar. No, I pray you; I'll not bereave you of your
  servant.
 Dio. Come, come;
I love the King your father and yourself
With more than foreign heart. We every day   35
Expect him here: when he shall come and find
Our paragon to all reports thus blasted,
He will repent the breadth of his great voyage,
Blame both my lord and me that we have taken
No care to your best courses. Go, I pray you,   40
Walk, and be cheerful once again; reserve
That excellent complexion which did steal
The eyes of young and old. Care not for me:
I can go home alone.
 Mar.   Well, I will go;   45
But yet I have no desire to it.
 Dio. Come, come, I know 'tis good for you.
Walk half an hour, Leonine, at the least.
Remember what I have said.
 Leon.   I warrant you, madam.   50
 Dio. I'll leave you, my sweet lady, for a while.
Pray, walk softly, do not heat your blood.
What! I must have care of you.

68. **wolt out:** wilt thou leave us.
69. **dropping industry:** industry undeterred by their dripping state.

Mar.   My thanks, sweet madam.
                                   [*Exit Dionyza.*]
Is this wind westerly that blows?   55
  Leon.   Southwest.
  Mar. When I was born, the wind was north.
  Leon.   Was't so?
  Mar. My father, as nurse says, did never fear,
But cried,"Good seamen!" to the sailors, galling   60
His kingly hands, haling ropes;
And, clasping to the mast, endured a sea
That almost burst the deck.
  Leon. When was this?
  Mar. When I was born: 65
Never was waves nor wind more violent;
And from the ladder tackle washes off
A canvas climber. "Ha!" says one, "wolt out?"
And with a dropping industry they skip
From stem to stern. The boatswain whistles, and   70
The master calls and trebles their confusion.
  Leon. Come, say your prayers.
  Mar. What mean you?
  Leon. If you require a little space for prayer,
I grant it. Pray: but be not tedious, for   75
The gods are quick of ear, and I am sworn
To do my work with haste.
  Mar.   Why will you kill me?
  Leon. To satisfy my lady.
  Mar. Why would she have me killed?   80
Now, as I can remember, by my troth,
I never did her hurt in all my life.
I never spake bad word, nor did ill turn

86. **against my will:** unintentionally.
89. **imply:** import; betoken.
93. **well favored:** fine looking.
100. **dispatch:** make haste about it.
103. **Half-part:** let's share equally.

To any living creature. Believe me, la,
I never killed a mouse nor hurt a fly.   85
I trod upon a worm against my will,
But I wept for it. How have I offended,
Wherein my death might yield her any profit,
Or my life imply her any danger?
 Leon. My commission   90
Is not to reason of the deed, but do't.
 Mar. You will not do't for all the world, I hope.
You are well favored, and your looks foreshow
You have a gentle heart. I saw you lately
When you caught hurt in parting two that fought.   95
Good sooth, it showed well in you! Do so now.
Your lady seeks my life: come you between
And save poor me, the weaker.
 Leon.   I am sworn,
And will dispatch.   [*He seizes her.*] 100

Enter Pirates.

1. Pir. Hold villain!   [*Leonine runs away.*]
2. Pir. A prize! a prize!
3. Pir. Half-part, mates, half-part. Come let's have
 her aboard suddenly.
     Exeunt [*Pirates with Marina*].

Enter Leonine.

Leon. These roguing thieves serve the great pirate 105
 Valdes;

[IV.ii.] In Mytilene, the pirates sell Marina to Boult, agent for a brothel. Delighted at such a prize, the brothel owners order Boult to advertise Marina's charms in the city to attract customers. Marina, horrified, is not comforted by the Bawd's description of what a fine life she will have. She resolves that she will die rather than lose her virginity.

Setting. **Mytilene:** on the island of Lesbos.

3. **narrowly:** thoroughly.

11-2. **If there be not a conscience to be used in every trade, we shall never prosper:** i.e., even our trade requires us to follow certain standards (employing healthy girls), if we are to prosper.

16. **to eleven, and brought them down again:** to the age of eleven, then debased them by making them harlots.

And they have seized Marina. Let her go:
There's no hope she will return. I'll swear she's dead
And thrown into the sea. But I'll see further.
Perhaps they will but please themselves upon her,   110
Not carry her aboard. If she remain,
Whom they have ravished must by me be slain.

Exit.

━━

[Scene II. Mytilene. A room in a brothel.]

Enter [Pander, Bawd, and Boult].

Pan. Boult!

Boult. Sir?

Pan. Search the market narrowly. Mytilene is full
of gallants. We lost too much money this mart by
being too wenchless.   5

Bawd. We were never so much out of creatures. We
have but poor three, and they can do no more than
they can do; and they with continual action are even
as good as rotten.

Pan. Therefore let's have fresh ones, whate'er we   10
pay for them. If there be not a conscience to be used
in every trade, we shall never prosper.

Bawd. Thou sayst true: 'tis not our bringing-up of
poor bastards—as, I think, I have brought up some
eleven.   15

Boult. Ay, to eleven, and brought them down again.
But shall I search the market?

20. sodden: stewed (referring to the steambath treatment for venereal disease).

25. roast: i.e., burned; that is, infected with venereal sores.

26. chequins: sequins, or zecchini, coins at one time used in both Italy and Turkey.

27. give over: retire.

29. get: make profit; possibly with a pun on "beget."

30-1. commodity: profit.

31. wages: balances.

34. hatched: closed; i.e., refuse to admit customers.

34-5. the sore terms we stand upon with the gods: our condition of having sorely displeased the gods.

38-9. no calling: i.e., not an occupation to which we were called by Providence, with reference to biblical injunctions to labor in the vocation to which one has been called.

43. gone through: made a deal.

Bawd. What else, man? The stuff we have, a strong wind will blow it to pieces, they are so pitifully sodden. 20

Pan. Thou sayest true; they're too unwholesome, o' conscience. The poor Transylvanian is dead, that lay with the little baggage.

Boult. Ay, she quickly pooped him: she made him roast meat for worms. But I'll go search the market. 25

Exit.

Pan. Three or four thousand chequins were as pretty a proportion to live quietly and so give over.

Bawd. Why to give over, I pray you? Is it a shame to get when we are old?

Pan. Oh, our credit comes not in like the commod- 30 ity, nor the commodity wages not with the danger: therefore, if in our youths we could pick up some pretty estate, 'twere not amiss to keep our door hatched. Besides, the sore terms we stand upon with the gods will be strong with us for giving o'er. 35

Bawd. Come, other sorts offend as well as we.

Pan. As well as we! Ay, and better too: we offend worse. Neither is our profession any trade: it's no call- ing. But here comes Boult.

Enter Boult, with the Pirates and Marina.

Boult. [*To Marina*] Come your ways.—My masters, 40 you say she's a virgin?

1. Pir. O sir, we doubt it not.

Boult. Master, I have gone through for this piece,

45. **earnest:** payment.
46. **qualities:** accomplishments; attractions.
48. **necessity:** lack.
51. **bated:** abated; decreased; **doit:** a coin of trifling value.
54. **presently:** at once.
55. **raw:** untutored; ignorant.
56. **entertainment:** employment.
70. **in:** for; in endowing her well.
72. **light:** fallen.
73. **like:** likely.

you see. If you like her, so; if not, I have lost my
earnest.   45

Bawd. Boult, has she any qualities?

Boult. She has a good face, speaks well, and has
excellent good clothes. There's no farther necessity of
qualities can make her be refused.

Bawd. What's her price, Boult?   50

Boult. I cannot be bated one doit of a thousand
pieces.

Pan. Well, follow me, my masters, you shall have
your money presently. Wife, take her in. Instruct her
what she has to do, that she may not be raw in her   55
entertainment.   [*Exeunt Pander and Pirates.*]

Bawd. Boult, take you the marks of her, the color
of her hair, complexion, height, her age, with warrant
of her virginity; and cry, "He that will give most shall
have her first." Such a maidenhead were no cheap   60
thing, if men were as they have been. Get this done as
I command you.

Boult. Performance shall follow.   *Exit.*

Mar. Alack that Leonine was so slack, so slow!
He should have struck, not spoke; or that these pirates,   65
Not enough barbarous, had not o'erboard thrown me
For to seek my mother!

Bawd. Why lament you, pretty one?

Mar. That I am pretty.

Bawd. Come, the gods have done their part in you.   70

Mar. I accuse them not.

Bawd. You are light into my hands, where you are
like to live.

Mar. The more my fault,

80. **difference:** variety; **complexions:** types of men, with reference to both appearance and disposition.

85. **honest:** chaste.

86. **Marry, whip thee:** plague take thee; **gosling:** fool.

87. **something to do:** trouble.

94. **cried:** advertised.

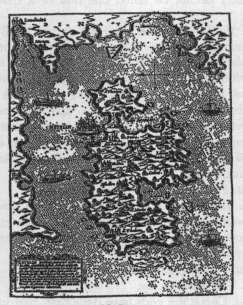

Mytilene.
From Giovanni Camocio, *Isole famose porti, fortezze, e terre maritime* (1574).

To 'scape his hands where I was like to die. 75

Bawd. Ay, and you shall live in pleasure.

Mar. No.

Bawd. Yes, indeed shall you, and taste gentlemen of all fashions. You shall fare well; you shall have the difference of all complexions. What! do you stop your 80 ears?

Mar. Are you a woman?

Bawd. What would you have me be, and I be not a woman?

Mar. An honest woman, or not a woman. 85

Bawd. Marry, whip thee, gosling. I think I shall have something to do with you. Come, you're a young foolish sapling and must be bowed as I would have you.

Mar. The gods defend me! 90

Bawd. If it please the gods to defend you by men, then men must comfort you, men must feed you, men must stir you up. Boult's returned.

[*Enter Boult.*]

Now, sir, hast thou cried her through the market?

Boult. I have cried her almost to the number of her 95 hairs. I have drawn her picture with my voice.

Bawd. And I prithee tell me, how dost thou find the inclination of the people, especially of the younger sort?

Boult. Faith, they listened to me as they would have 100 hearkened to their father's testament. There was a

108. Verolles: French *verolés*, pox.

109. offered: tried.

113. repair: strengthen.

114. in our shadow: under our disreputable roof; **crowns:** coins, but there is probably a pun on the idea that venereal disease often resulted in a bald crown; **the sun:** possibly the house was known as the Sun, a common tavern name, particularly associated with disreputable houses, the sun sign being symbolic of sexual passion.

116. this sign: i.e., Marina, whose sign would be Virgo, the Virgin. Compare *Cymbeline*, I.ii.31: "She's a good sign."

123. mere: downright.

127. present practice: immediate experience.

129-30. which is her way to go with warrant: which she has been licensed to go by marriage.

Spaniard's mouth watered and he went to bed to her
very description.

Bawd. We shall have him here tomorrow with his
best ruff on.   105

Boult. Tonight, tonight. But, mistress, do you know
the French knight that cowers i' the hams?

Bawd. Who, Monsieur Verolles?

Boult. Ay, he. He offered to cut a caper at the proc-
lamation; but he made a groan at it and swore he   110
would see her tomorrow.

Bawd. Well, well: as for him, he brought his disease
hither. Here he does but repair it. I know he will come
in our shadow, to scatter his crowns in the sun.

Boult. Well, if we had of every nation a traveler,   115
we should lodge them with this sign.

Bawd. [*To Marina*] Pray you, come hither awhile.
You have fortunes coming upon you. Mark me: you
must seem to do that fearfully which you commit will-
ingly, despise profit where you have most gain. To   120
weep that you live as ye do makes pity in your lovers.
Seldom but that pity begets you a good opinion, and
that opinion a mere profit.

Mar. I understand you not.

Boult. O, take her home, mistress, take her home.   125
These blushes of hers must be quenched with some
present practice.

Bawd. Thou sayest true, i' faith, so they must; for
your bride goes to that with shame which is her way
to go with warrant.   130

Boult. Faith, some do, and some do not. But, mistress, if I have bargained for the joint—

140-41. custom: business. The implication is that besides the profit Marina will bring, which he will share, Boult is assured that he may enjoy Marina himself but must resign himself to sharing her.

142. a good turn: equivocal: good fortune and a "good turn in the bed," sexual pleasure.

142-43. say what a paragon she is, and thou hast the harvest out of thine own report: you will profit by advertising her extraordinary qualities.

━━━━━━━━━━━━━━━━━━━━━━━━━━━━━

[IV.iii.] Cleon rebukes Dionyza for the murder of Marina but is finally reconciled to the fact. Dionyza points out that, since she has disposed of Leonine by poison, no one can know how Marina died, and their mourning, emphasized by the monument they are erecting to her memory, will safeguard them from suspicion.

Bawd. Thou mayst cut a morsel off the spit.

Boult. I may so.

Bawd. Who should deny it? Come, young one, I like 135
the manner of your garments well.

Boult. Ay, by my faith, they shall not be changed
yet.

Bawd. Boult, spend thou that in the town. Report
what a sojourner we have: you'll lose nothing by cus- 140
tom. When Nature framed this piece, she meant thee
a good turn: therefore say what a paragon she is, and
thou hast the harvest out of thine own report.

Boult. I warrant you, mistress, thunder shall not so
awake the beds of eels as my giving out her beauty 145
stirs up the lewdly-inclined. I'll bring home some tonight.

Bawd. Come your ways: follow me.

Mar. If fires be hot, knives sharp, or water deep,
Untied I still my virgin knot will keep.   150
Diana, aid my purpose!

Bawd. What have we to do with Diana? Pray you,
will you go with us?

Exeunt.

[Scene III. Tarsus. A room in the Governor's house.]

Enter Cleon and Dionyza.

Dio. Why, are you foolish? Can it be undone?

Cleon. O Dionyza, such a piece of slaughter

8. Much less in blood than virtue: i.e., Marina's nobility of character more truly entitles her to be called a lady than even her high birth.

10. I' the justice of compare: in honest comparison.

12. drunk to him: tasted the drink before him.

13. fact: crime. Cleon implies that it would have been well if she had killed herself with the same poison.

16. it: the child; i.e., nurses have not the Fates' power to determine when a child shall die.

17. cross: contradict.

19. honest attribute: honorable reputation.

21. go to: say no more.

27. strain: descent; blood.

30. but: only.

31. prime: original; **consent:** complicity.

The sun and moon ne'er looked upon!
  Dion.   I think
You'll turn a child again.   5
  Cleon. Were I chief lord of all this spacious world,
I'd give it to undo the deed.—O lady,
Much less in blood than virtue, yet a princess
To equal any single crown o' the earth
I' the justice of compare!—O villain Leonine!   10
Whom thou hast poisoned too:
If thou hadst drunk to him, 't had been a kindness
Becoming well thy fact. What canst thou say
When noble Pericles shall demand his child?
  Dion. That she is dead. Nurses are not the Fates,   15
To foster it, nor ever to preserve.
She died at night: I'll say so. Who can cross it?
Unless you play the pious innocent
And for an honest attribute cry out,
"She died by foul play."   20
  Cleon.   Oh, go to. Well, well,
Of all the faults beneath the heavens the gods
Do like this worst.
  Dion.   Be one of those that thinks
The petty wrens of Tarsus will fly hence   25
And open this to Pericles. I do shame
To think of what a noble strain you are
And of how coward a spirit.
  Cleon.   To such proceeding
Who ever but his approbation added,   30
Though not his prime consent, he did not flow
From honorable sources.
  Dion.   Be it so, then.

36. **distain:** blemish (by comparison).

39. **blurted:** snorted; **held a mawkin:** considered a slattern.

40. **thorough:** through.

43. **greets:** pleases.

50. **characters:** letters.

53. **harpy:** the mythological harpy allured men with her beautiful woman's face, only to snatch them away.

56. **superstitiously:** with extreme caution.

57. **winter:** i.e., disclaiming personal responsibility.

Harpies.
From Vincenzo Cartari, *Le imagini de gl' dei de gli antichi* (1609).

Yet none does know but you how she came dead,
Nor none can know, Leonine being gone. 35
She did distain my child and stood between
Her and her fortunes. None would look on her
But cast their gazes on Marina's face,
Whilst ours was blurted at and held a mawkin,
Not worth the time of day. It pierced me thorough; 40
And though you call my course unnatural,
You not your child well loving, yet I find
It greets me as an enterprise of kindness
Performed to your sole daughter.

 Cleon.   Heavens forgive it! 45
 Dio. And as for Pericles,
What should he say? We wept after her hearse,
And yet we mourn. Her monument
Is almost finished, and her epitaphs
In glitt'ring golden characters express 50
A general praise to her and care in us
At whose expense 'tis done.

 Cleon.   Thou art like the harpy,
Which, to betray, dost, with thine angel's face,
Seize with thine eagle's talons. 55

 Dion. You are like one that superstitiously
Do swear to the gods that winter kills the flies:
But yet I know you'll do as I advise.

           [Exeunt.]

[IV.iv.] Gower reports how Pericles has voyaged to Tarsus to see Marina. A dumb show portrays him being shown his daughter's tomb and departing again. Gower relates that the sorrowing Pericles rides out another storm. Attention is now directed to Marina's fortunes in Mytilene.

▬▬▬▬▬▬▬▬▬▬▬▬

1. **waste:** destroy.
2. **cockles:** cockle shells.
3. **Making:** traveling.
6. **several:** different.
8. **gaps:** intervals.
10. **thwarting:** crossing.
16. **in time:** opportunely.
18. **think his pilot Thought:** consider that he is piloted by thought.
19. **with his steerage shall your thoughts grow on:** with Thought conducting you, shall you travel over time and space.
22. **Your ears unto your eyes I'll reconcile:** I will tell you the meaning of what you see.

[Scene IV.]

Enter Gower, [before the monument of Marina at Tarsus].

Thus time we waste and longest leagues make short;
Sail seas in cockles, have and wish but for't;
Making, to take your imagination,
From bourn to bourn, region to region.
By you being pardoned, we commit no crime   5
To use one language in each several clime
Where our scenes seems to live. I do beseech you
To learn of me, who stand i' the gaps to teach you
The stages of our story. Pericles
Is now again thwarting the wayward seas,   10
Attended on by many a lord and knight,
To see his daughter, all his life's delight.
Old Helicanus goes along. Behind
Is left to govern it, you bear in mind,
Old Escanes, whom Helicanus late   15
Advanced in time to great and high estate.
Well-sailing ships and bounteous winds have brought
This king to Tarsus—think his pilot Thought;
So with his steerage shall your thoughts grow on—
To fetch his daughter home, who first is gone.   20
Like motes and shadows see them move awhile.
Your ears unto your eyes I'll reconcile.

[Dumb Show.]

23. **suffer by foul show:** be injured by false appearances.

24. **borrowed passion:** assumed grief; **old:** great.

32. **wit:** learn.

40. **Thetis:** a sea-goddess; **proud:** with a secondary sense "swollen."

45. **she:** Thetis.

Thetis.
From Geoffrey Whitney, *A Choice of Emblems* (1586).

*Enter Pericles, at one door, with all his train, Cleon
and Dionyza at the other. Cleon shows Pericles the
tomb, whereat Pericles makes lamentation, puts on
sackcloth, and in a mighty passion departs.* [*Then
exeunt Cleon, Dionyza, and the rest.*]

See how belief may suffer by foul show!
This borrowed passion stands for true old woe;
And Pericles, in sorrow all devoured,   25
With sighs shot through and biggest tears o'ershow-
    ered,
Leaves Tarsus and again embarks. He swears
Never to wash his face nor cut his hairs:
He puts on sackcloth and to sea. He bears   30
A tempest, which his mortal vessel tears,
And yet he rides it out. Now please you wit
The epitaph is for Marina writ
By wicked Dionyza.
    [*Reads the inscription on Marina's monument.*]
    "The fairest, sweet'st, and best lies here,   35
        Who withered in her spring of year.
    She was of Tyrus the King's daughter,
        On whom foul Death hath made this slaughter.
    Marina was she called; and at her birth,
    Thetis, being proud, swallowed some part o' the   40
        earth.
    Therefore the earth, fearing to be o'erflowed,
    Hath Thetis' birth child on the Heavens be-
        stowed:
    Wherefore she does, and swears she'll never stint,   45
    Make raging battery upon shores of flint."

47. **visor:** mask.
50. **bear:** allow; **courses:** actions.

––––––––––––––––––––––––––

[IV.v.] Two gentlemen leave the brothel, where Marina has lectured them and destroyed their taste for fleshly pleasure.

––––––––––––––––––––––––––

4. **divinity:** theology.
7. **Shall's:** shall we; **vestals:** properly, devotees of the goddess Vesta (Greek Hestia), used loosely for virgin priestesses.

A notorious brothel in Paris Garden, Southwark. From Nicholas Goodman, *Holland's Leaguer* (1632).

No visor does become black villainy
So well as soft and tender flattery.
Let Pericles believe his daughter's dead
And bear his courses to be ordered   50
By Lady Fortune; while our scene must play
His daughter's woe and heavy welladay
In her unholy service. Patience, then,
And think you now are all in Mytilen.

                              Exit.

[Scene V. Mytilene. A street before the brothel.]

Enter, [from the brothel,] two Gentlemen.

1. Gent. Did you ever hear the like?

2. Gent. No, nor never shall do in such a place as
this, she being once gone.

1. Gent. But to have divinity preached there! Did
you ever dream of such a thing?   5

2. Gent. No, no. Come, I am for no more bawdy
houses. Shall's go hear the vestals sing?

1. Gent. I'll do anything now that is virtuous; but
I am out of the road of rutting forever.

                            Exeunt.

[IV.vi.] The brothel owners are in despair at Marina's refusal to perform her duties. Lysimachus, Governor of the country, comes in disguise and is left with Marina. Impressed by Marina's beauty and virtue, Lysimachus gives her gold and promises to protect her. The Bawd and Boult, irate that she has repulsed Lysimachus, decide that she must be deflowered and made fit for her employment. Marina even lectures Boult effectively, however, and convinces him that she might be a source of profit by giving lessons in music and other skills. Boult promises to seek the consent of his master and mistress.

<hr/>

4. **Priapus:** god of fruitfulness, whose likenesses were characterized by an abnormally large phallus.

6. **fitment:** appropriate service; **do me the kindness:** perform the natural act. **Me** with the verbs throughout the speech indicates the ethical dative construction.

9. **cheapen:** bargain for.

12. **cavalleria:** gallants; **swearers:** devoted customers.

13. **the pox upon:** plague take; **green sickness:** an anemia afflicting maidens.

15. **the pox:** syphilis.

17. **lown:** lout.

18. **peevish:** perverse.

19. **How a dozen:** how much for a dozen.

20. **to-bless:** thoroughly bless, **to** being an intensive.

[Scene VI. Mytilene. A room in the brothel.]

Enter [Pander, Bawd, and Boult].

Pan. Well, I had rather than twice the worth of her she had ne'er come here.

Bawd. Fie, fie upon her! She's able to freeze the god Priapus and undo a whole generation. We must either get her ravished or be rid of her. When she should do 5 for clients her fitment and do me the kindness of our profession, she has me her quirks, her reasons, her master reasons, her prayers, her knees; that she would make a Puritan of the Devil, if he should cheapen a kiss of her. 10

Boult. Faith, I must ravish her, or she'll disfurnish us of all our cavalleria and make our swearers priests.

Pan. Now, the pox upon her green sickness for me!

Bawd. Faith, there's no way to be rid on't but by the way to the pox. Here comes the Lord Lysimachus dis- 15 guised.

Boult. We should have both lord and lown, if the peevish baggage would but give way to customers.

Enter Lysimachus.

Lys. How now! How a dozen of virginities?

Bawd. Now, the gods to-bless your Honor! 20

Boult. I am glad to see your Honor in good health.

Lys. You may so. 'Tis the better for you that your resorters stand upon sound legs. How now, wholesome

24. **that:** one that, or that which.

35. **but:** what Boult thinks of is "a prick," referring to the proverbial idea that every rose has a thorn.

39. **gives a good report to a number to be chaste:** gives a number of people an undeserved reputation for chastity.

43-4. **she would serve after a long voyage at sea:** an ironical understatement.

45. **give me leave a word:** allow me a brief word with her.

iniquity? Have you that a man may deal withal and
defy the surgeon?   25

Bawd. We have here one, sir, if she would—but
there never came her like in Mytilene.

Lys. If she'd do the deeds of darkness, thou wouldst
say.

Bawd. Your Honor knows what 'tis to say well   30
enough.

Lys. Well, call forth, call forth.

Boult. For flesh and blood, sir, white and red, you
shall see a rose; and she were a rose indeed, if she had
but—   35

Lys. What, prithee?

Boult. O sir, I can be modest.

Lys. That dignifies the renown of a bawd, no less
than it gives a good report to a number to be chaste.

                                          [*Exit Boult.*]

Bawd. Here comes that which grows to the stalk;   40
never plucked yet, I can assure you.

[*Enter Boult with Marina.*]

Is she not a fair creature?

Lys. Faith, she would serve after a long voyage at
sea. Well, there's for you. Leave us.

Bawd. I beseech your Honor, give me leave a word, 45
and I'll have done presently.

Lys. I beseech you, do.

Bawd. [*To Marina*] First, I would have you note,
this is an honorable man.

50-1. worthily note him: put him down as worthy.

57. virginal fencing: defense of your virginity.

60. graciously: virtuously.

63. paced: taught her paces; tamed.

64. manage: management, as of a horse.

74. gamester: harlot.

Mar. I desire to find him so, that I may worthily 50
note him.

Bawd. Next, he's the Governor of this country, and
a man whom I am bound to.

Mar. If he govern the country, you are bound to
him indeed. But how honorable he is in that, I know 55
not.

Bawd. Pray you, without any more virginal fencing,
will you use him kindly? He will line your apron with
gold.

Mar. What he will do graciously, I will thankfully 60
receive.

Lys. Ha' you done?

Bawd. My lord, she's not paced yet: you must take
some pains to work her to your manage. Come, we
will leave His Honor and her together. Go thy ways. 65

[*Exeunt Bawd, Pander, and Boult.*]

Lys. Now, pretty one, how long have you been at
this trade?

Mar. What trade, sir?

Lys. Why, I cannot name't but I shall offend.

Mar. I cannot be offended with my trade. Please 70
you to name it.

Lys. How long have you been of this profession?

Mar. E'er since I can remember.

Lys. Did you go to't so young? Were you a gamester
at five or at seven? 75

Mar. Earlier too, sir, if now I be one.

Lys. Why, the house you dwell in proclaims you
to be a creature of sale.

Mar. Do you know this house to be a place of such

81. **parts:** qualities.

82. **principal:** superior.

89. **authority:** i.e., as a magistrate who should punish vice.

93. **If put upon you:** if honor has been conferred upon you; **make the judgment good:** confirm the judgment.

109. **clear:** pure.

resort and will come into't? I hear say you are of   80
honorable parts and are the Governor of this place.

Lys. Why, hath your principal made known unto
you who I am?

Mar. Who is my principal?

Lys. Why, your herbwoman; she that sets seeds and   85
roots of shame and iniquity. Oh, you have heard
something of my power and so stand aloof for more
serious wooing. But I protest to thee, pretty one, my
authority shall not see thee, or else look friendly upon
thee. Come, bring me to some private place: come,   90
come.

Mar. If you were born to honor, show it now.
If put upon you, make the judgment good
That thought you worthy of it.

Lys. How's this? how's this? Some more: be sage.   95
Mar.   For me
That am a maid—though most ungentle fortune
Have placed me in this sty, where, since I came,
Diseases have been sold dearer than physic—
Oh, that the gods   100
Would set me free from this unhallowed place,
Though they did change me to the meanest bird
That flies i' the purer air!

Lys.   I did not think
Thou couldst have spoke so well; ne'er dreamt thou   105
    couldst.
Had I brought hither a corrupted mind,
Thy speech had altered it. Hold, here's gold for thee.
Persever in that clear way thou goest,
And the gods strengthen thee!   110

115. piece: masterpiece.

122. doorkeeper: a term for a pander, who prevents interruption of a customer's pleasure.

127. cope: sky.

Mar.   The good gods preserve you!
Lys. For me, be you thoughten
That I came with no ill intent; for to me
The very doors and windows savor vilely.
Fare thee well. Thou art a piece of virtue, and   115
I doubt not but thy training hath been noble.
Hold, here's more gold for thee.
A curse upon him, die he like a thief,
That robs thee of thy goodness! If thou dost
Hear from me, it shall be for thy good.   120

[*Enter Boult.*]

Boult. I beseech your Honor, one piece for me.
Lys. Avaunt, thou damned doorkeeper!
Your house, but for this virgin that doth prop it,
Would sink and overwhelm you. Away!   [*Exit.*]
Boult. How's this? We must take another course 125
with you. If your peevish chastity, which is not worth
a breakfast in the cheapest country under the cope,
shall undo a whole household, let me be gelded like
a spaniel. Come your ways.
Mar. Whither would you have me?   130
Boult. I must have your maidenhead taken off, or
the common hangman shall execute it. Come your
ways. We'll have no more gentlemen driven away.
Come your ways, I say.

Enter Bawd.

Bawd. How now! what's the matter?   135

146. Crack the glass of her virginity: compare the proverb "Glasses and lasses are brittle ware" (fragile and easily destroyed).

154. Marry, come up: hoity toity!

155. with rosemary and bays: rosemary and bay leaves were traditional garnishes for festive occasions; hence Marina is accused of making a great show of her chastity.

162. my master: i.e., as low a wretch as my master.

165. they do better thee in their command: they are superior to you in giving orders that you have to follow.

166. pained'st: most tortured.

Boult. Worse and worse, mistress: she has here spoken holy words to the Lord Lysimachus.

Bawd. Oh, abominable!

Boult. She makes our profession as it were to stink afore the face of the gods. 140

Bawd. Marry, hang her up forever!

Boult. The nobleman would have dealt with her like a nobleman, and she sent him away as cold as a snowball, saying his prayers too.

Bawd. Boult, take her away. Use her at thy pleas- 145 ure. Crack the glass of her virginity and make the rest malleable.

Boult. And if she were a thornier piece of ground than she is, she shall be plowed.

Mar. Hark, hark, you gods! 150

Bawd. She conjures. Away with her! Would she had never come within my doors! Marry, hang you! She's born to undo us. Will you not go the way of womenkind? Marry, come up, my dish of chastity with rosemary and bays! [*Exit.*] 155

Boult. Come, mistress: come your ways with me.

Mar. Whither wilt thou have me?

Boult. To take from you the jewel you hold so dear.

Mar. Prithee, tell me one thing first.

Boult. Come now, your one thing. 160

Mar. What canst thou wish thine enemy to be?

Boult. Why, I could wish him to be my master, or, rather, my mistress.

Mar. Neither of these are so bad as thou art,
Since they do better thee in their command. 165
Thou holdst a place for which the pained'st fiend

167. **in reputation:** so far as reputation goes.

169. **Coistrel:** base fellow; **Tib:** a common name for a harlot.

178. **common shores:** gutters.

181. **professest:** make a career of.

182. **own a name too dear:** think himself too good for.

187. **keep from boast:** not boast of.

Of hell would not in reputation change.
Thou art the damned doorkeeper to every
Coistrel that comes inquiring for his Tib.
To the choleric fisting of every rogue   170
Thy ear is liable. Thy food is such
As hath been belched on by infected lungs.

   Boult. What would you have me do? Go to the
wars, would you? where a man may serve seven years
for the loss of a leg, and have not money enough in 175
the end to buy him a wooden one?

   Mar. Do anything but this thou doest. Empty
Old receptacles, or common shores, of filth;
Serve by indenture to the common hangman.
Any of these ways are yet better than this;   180
For what thou professest a baboon, could he speak,
Would own a name too dear. Oh, that the gods
Would safely deliver me from this place!
Here, here's gold for thee.
If that thy master would gain by me,   185
Proclaim that I can sing, weave, sew, and dance,
With other virtues which I'll keep from boast;
And I will undertake all these to teach.
I doubt not but this populous city will
Yield many scholars.   190

   Boult. But can you teach all this you speak of?

   Mar. Prove that I cannot, take me home again
And prostitute me to the basest groom
That doth frequent your house.

   Boult. Well, I will see what I can do for thee. If I 195
can place thee, I will.

   Mar. But amongst honest women.

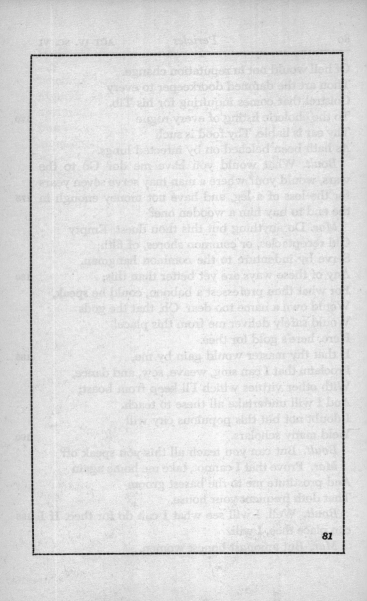

Boult. Faith, my acquaintance lies little amongst them. But since my master and mistress have bought you, there's no going but by their consent. Therefore 200 I will make them acquainted with your purpose, and I doubt not but I shall find them tractable enough. Come, I'll do for thee what I can. Come your ways.

Exeunt.

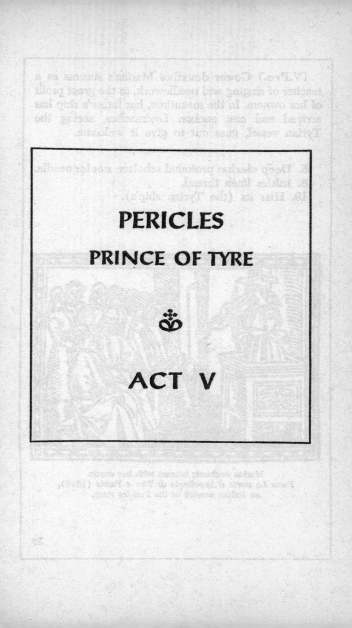

PERICLES

PRINCE OF TYRE

ACT V

[V.Pro.] Gower describes Marina's success as a teacher of singing and needlework, to the great profit of her owners. In the meantime, her father's ship has arrived and cast anchor. Lysimachus, seeing the Tyrian vessel, goes out to give it welcome.

5. **Deep clerks:** profound scholars; **neele:** needle.
8. **inkle:** linen thread.
19. **His:** its (the Tyrian ship's).

Marina enchants hearers with her music.
From *La storia d'Appollonia di Tiro e Tarsia* (1616),
an Italian version of the Pericles story.

[ACT V]

Enter Gower [as Prologue].

Marina thus the brothel 'scapes and chances
Into an honest house, our story says.
She sings like one immortal, and she dances
As goddess-like to her admired lays;
Deep clerks she dumbs, and with her neele composes 5
Nature's own shape, of bud, bird, branch, or berry,
That even her art sisters the natural roses;
Her inkle, silk, twin with the rubied cherry:
That pupils lacks she none of noble race,
Who pour their bounty on her, and her gain 10
She gives the cursed bawd. Here we her place;
And to her father turn our thoughts again,
Where we left him, on the sea. We there him lost:
Whence, driven before the winds, he is arrived
Here where his daughter dwells; and on this coast 15
Suppose him now at anchor. The city strived
God Neptune's annual feast to keep: from whence
Lysimachus our Tyrian ship espies,
His banners sable, trimmed with rich expense;
And to him in his barge with fervor hies. 20
In your supposing once more put your sight

22. **heavy:** sorrowful.

23-4. Where what is done in action, more, if might,/ Shall be discovered: where what happens shall be more fully revealed in action insofar as possible.

▬▬▬▬▬▬▬▬▬▬▬▬▬▬▬▬▬▬▬▬▬

[V.i.] Helicanus welcomes Lysimachus aboard the ship but warns him that Pericles is sunk in sorrow and will neither eat nor speak to anyone. Lysimachus suggests that Marina may be successful in rousing Pericles from his lethargy and has her brought aboard. Pericles, at first taking no notice of Marina, is struck by her mention of her noble parentage. When she has told her story in full, Pericles joyfully acknowledges her to be his daughter. Lulled by mysterious music, Pericles slumbers. In a vision the goddess Diana appears to him and orders him to relate his story at her temple at Ephesus.

▬▬▬▬▬▬▬▬▬▬▬▬▬▬▬▬▬▬▬▬▬

2. **resolve:** inform.
12. **fairly:** graciously.

Of heavy Pericles. Think this his bark,
Where what is done in action, more, if might,
Shall be discovered. Please you, sit, and hark.

                                        Exit.

━━━━━━━━━━━━━━━━━━━━━━━━━━━━━━━━━━━━━

[Scene I. On board Pericles' ship, off Mytilene.

A close pavilion on deck, with a curtain before it;
    Pericles within it, reclined on a couch; a
    barge lying beside the Tyrian vessel.]

*Enter Helicanus, to him two Sailors, [one belonging
    to the Tyrian vessel, the other to the barge].*

Tyr. Sail. [*To the Sailor of Mytilene*] Where is
    Lord Helicanus? He can resolve you.
Oh, here he is.
Sir, there is a barge put off from Mytilene,
And in it is Lysimachus, the Governor,   5
Who craves to come aboard. What is your will?
Hel. That he have his. Call up some gentlemen.
Tyr. Sail. Ho, gentlemen! my lord calls.

            Enter two or three Gentlemen.

1. Gent. Doth your Lordship call?
Hel. Gentlemen, there is some of worth would come   10
    aboard.
I pray, greet him fairly.

14. **would:** wish.
16. **reverend:** revered.
30. **prorogue:** prolong.
31. **Upon what ground is his distemperature:** what is the cause of his disturbance.
37. **bootless:** unprofitable.

[*The Gentlemen and the two Sailors descend and go
on board the barge.*]

[*Enter from the barge Lysimachus and Lords, with
the Gentlemen and the two Sailors.*]

Tyr. Sail. Sir,
This is the man that can, in aught you would,
Resolve you.   15
    Lys. Hail, reverend sir! the gods preserve you!
    Hel. And you, sir, to outlive the age I am
And die as I would do.
    Lys.   You wish me well.
Being on shore, honoring of Neptune's triumphs,   20
Seeing this goodly vessel ride before us,
I made to it, to know of whence you are.
    Hel. First, what is your place?
    Lys.   I am the Governor
Of this place you lie before.   25
    Hel. Sir,
Our vessel is of Tyre, in it the King;
A man who for this three months hath not spoken
To anyone, nor taken sustenance
But to prorogue his grief.   30
    Lys. Upon what ground is his distemperature?
    Hel. 'Twould be too tedious to repeat;
But the main grief springs from the loss
Of a beloved daughter and a wife.
    Lys. May we not see him?   35
    Hel. You may;
But bootless is your sight: he will not speak
To any.

42. **mortal:** fatal.

51. **questionless:** undoubtedly.

52. **chosen:** choice.

55. **all happy as the fairest of all:** i.e., as fortunately endowed in every way as she is the fairest of all.

60. **bears recovery's name:** is termed a remedy.

63. **want:** need.

64. **weary for the staleness:** i.e., tired of the same diet.

67. **graff:** graft; plant.

Lys. Yet let me obtain my wish.

Hel. Behold him. [*Pericles discovered.*] This was   40
    a goodly person
Till the disaster that, one mortal night,
Drove him to this.

Lys. Sir King, all hail! The gods preserve you!
Hail royal sir!   45

Hel. It is in vain: he will not speak to you.

1. Lord. Sir,
We have a maid in Mytilene, I durst wager,
Would win some words of him.

Lys.   'Tis well bethought.   50
She, questionless, with her sweet harmony
And other chosen attractions, would allure,
And make a batt'ry through his deafened parts,
Which now are midway stopped.
She is all happy as the fairest of all,   55
And with her fellow maids is now upon
The leafy shelter that abuts against
The island's side.

    [*Whispers a Lord, who goes off in the barge of
                        Lysimachus.*]

Hel. Sure, all effectless; yet nothing we'll omit
That bears recovery's name. But, since your kindness   60
We have stretched thus far, let us beseech you
That for our gold we may provision have,
Wherein we are not destitute for want
But weary for the staleness.

Lys.   O sir, a courtesy   65
Which if we should deny, the most just God
For every graff would send a caterpillar

69. **at large:** in full.

75. **goodly presence:** handsome person.

76. **gallant:** lovely.

78. **gentle kind:** wellborn family.

82. **prosperous and artificial feat:** successful skill of performance.

84. **sacred physic:** devoted healing.

89. **suffered:** permitted.

And so inflict our province. Yet once more
Let me entreat to know at large the cause
Of your King's sorrow. 70
    Hel.   Sit, sir, I will recount it to you.
But, see, I am prevented.

[*Enter, from the barge, Lord, with Marina, and a
young Lady.*]

    Lys.   Oh, here's
The lady that I sent for. Welcome, fair one!—
Is't not a goodly presence? 75
    Hel.   She's a gallant lady.
    Lys. She's such a one, that, were I well assured
Came of a gentle kind and noble stock,
I'd wish no better choice, and think me rarely wed.
Fair one, all goodness that consists in bounty 80
Expect even here, where is a kingly patient.
If that thy prosperous and artificial feat
Can draw him but to answer thee in aught,
Thy sacred physic shall receive such pay
As thy desires can wish. 85
    Mar.   Sir, I will use
My utmost skill in his recovery, provided
That none but I and my companion maid
Be suffered to come near him.
    Lys.   Come, let us leave her; 90
And the gods make her prosperous!   [*Marina sings.*]
    Lys. Marked he your music?
    Mar.   No, nor looked on us.

102. malign: treat with hostility.

105. rooted out my parentage: destroyed my parents.

106. the world and awkward casualties: the unfortunate chances of the world.

Lys. See, she will speak to him.

Mar. Hail, sir! My lord, lend ear. 95

Per. Hum, ha! [*Averts his face.*]

Mar. I am a maid,
My lord, that ne'er before invited eyes
But have been gazed on like a comet. She speaks,
My lord, that, may be, hath endured a grief 100
Might equal yours, if both were justly weighed.
Though wayward Fortune did malign my state,
My derivation was from ancestors
Who stood equivalent with mighty kings:
But Time hath rooted out my parentage 105
And to the world and awkward casualties
Bound me in servitude. [*Aside*] I will desist;
But there is something glows upon my cheek,
And whispers in mine ear, "Go not till he speak."

Per. My fortunes—parentage—good parentage— 110
To equal mine!—Was it not thus? What say you?

Mar. I said, my lord, if you did know my parentage,
You would not do me violence.

Per. I do think so. Pray you, turn your eyes upon me.
You are like something that—What countrywoman? 115
Here of these shores?

Mar.   No, nor of any shores.
Yet I was mortally brought forth and am
No other than I appear.

Per. I am great with woe and shall deliver weeping. 120
My dearest wife was like this maid, and such a one
My daughter might have been: my queen's square
     brows;
Her stature to an inch; as wandlike straight,

134. **to owe:** by your possession of them.
136. **in the reporting:** even as they are spoken.
151. **opened:** revealed.

As silver-voiced; her eyes as jewel-like 125
And cased as richly; in pace another Juno;
Who starves the ears she feeds and makes them
  hungry,
The more she gives them speech. Where do you live?

Mar. Where I am but a stranger. From the deck 130
You may discern the place.

Per.   Where were you bred?
And how achieved you these endowments, which
You make more rich to owe?

Mar. If I should tell my history, it would seem 135
Like lies disdained in the reporting.

Per.   Prithee, speak.
Falseness cannot come from thee, for thou lookest
Modest as Justice and thou seemst a palace
For the crowned Truth to dwell in. I will believe thee 140
And make my senses credit thy relation
To points that seem impossible, for thou lookest
Like one I loved indeed. What were thy friends?
Didst thou not say, when I did push thee back—
Which was when I perceived thee—that thou camest 145
From good descending?

Mar.   So indeed I did.

Per. Report thy parentage. I think thou saidst
Thou hadst been tossed from wrong to injury,
And that thou thoughtst thy griefs might equal mine, 150
If both were opened.

Mar.   Some such thing
I said, and said no more but what my thoughts
Did warrant me was likely.

159. graves: funeral monuments.

159-60. smiling/ Extremity out of act: mastering desperation with a smile.

181-82. fairy/ Motion: a puppet made by fairies; folklore credited fairies with substituting such puppets for human babies.

Patience personified.
From Cesare Ripa, *Iconologia* (1603).

Per.   Tell thy story: 155
If thine considered prove the thousandth part
Of my endurance, thou art a man and I
Have suffered like a girl. Yet thou dost look
Like Patience gazing on kings' graves and smiling
Extremity out of act. What were thy friends? 160
How lost thou them? Thy name, my most kind virgin?
Recount, I do beseech thee. Come, sit by me.
 Mar. My name is Marina.
 Per.   Oh, I am mocked,
And thou by some incensed god sent hither 165
To make the world to laugh at me.
 Mar.   Patience, good sir,
Or here I'll cease.
 Per. Nay, I'll be patient.
Thou little knowst how thou dost startle me, 170
To call thyself Marina.
 Mar.   The name
Was given me by one that had some power,
My father, and a king.
 Per.   How! a king's daughter? 175
And called Marina?
 Mar.   You said you would believe me;
But, not to be a troubler of your peace,
I will end here.
 Per. But are you flesh and blood? 180
Have you a working pulse? and are no fairy
Motion? Well, speak on: where were you born?
And wherefore called Marina?
 Mar.   Called Marina
For I was born at sea.   185

190. **Delivered:** reported.

197-98. **give o'er:** cease.

199. **by the syllable:** to the last syllable.

200. **give me leave:** pardon me.

208. **Whither will you have me:** what will you have me say.

Per.   At sea! What mother?

  Mar. My mother was the daughter of a king;
Who died the minute I was born,
As my good nurse Lychorida hath oft
Delivered weeping.   190

  Per.   Oh, stop there a little!
[*Aside*] This is the rarest dream that e'er dull sleep
Did mock sad fools withal. This cannot be
My daughter buried.—Well, where were you bred?
I'll hear you more, to the bottom of your story,   195
And never interrupt you.

  Mar. You scorn. Believe me, 'twere best I did give
    o'er.

  Per. I will believe you by the syllable
Of what you shall deliver. Yet, give me leave.   200
How came you in these parts? Where were you bred?

  Mar. The King my father did in Tarsus leave me;
Till cruel Cleon, with his wicked wife,
Did seek to murder me: and having wooed
A villain to attempt it, who having drawn to do't,   205
A crew of pirates came and rescued me,
Brought me to Mytilene. But, good sir,
Whither will you have me? Why do you weep? It may
    be,
You think me an impostor. No, good faith: 210
I am the daughter to King Pericles,
If good King Pericles be.

  Per. Ho, Helicanus!

  Hel. Calls my lord?

  Per. Thou art a grave and noble counselor,   215
Most wise in general: tell me, if thou canst,

What this maid is, or what is like to be,
That thus hath made me weep.
    Hel.   I know not: but
Here is the regent, sir, of Mytilene,   220
Speaks nobly of her.
    Lys.   She never would tell
Her parentage: being demanded that,
She would sit still and weep.
    Per. O Helicanus, strike me, honored sir;   225
Give me a gash, put me to present pain;
Lest this great sea of joys rushing upon me
O'erbear the shores of my mortality
And drown me with their sweetness. Oh, come hither,
Thou that begetst him that did thee beget;   230
Thou that wast born at sea, buried at Tarsus,
And found at sea again! O Helicanus,
Down on thy knees; thank the holy gods as loud
As thunder threatens us. This is Marina.
What was thy mother's name? Tell me but that,   235
For truth can never be confirmed enough,
Though doubts did ever sleep.
    Mar.   First, sir, I pray,
What is your title?
    Per. I am Pericles of Tyre: but tell me now   240
My drowned queen's name, as in the rest you said
Thou hast been godlike perfect, the heir of kingdoms,
And another life to Pericles thy father.
    Mar. Is it no more to be your daughter than
To say my mother's name was Thaisa?   245
Thaisa was my mother, who did end
The minute I began.

252. justify in knowledge: knowingly confirm.
258. wild in my beholding: overjoyed at what I see.
262. sure: certainly.
274. answer to: accord with; **just:** honest.

Per. Now, blessing on thee! Rise: thou art my child.
Give me fresh garments. Mine own, Helicanus!
She is not dead at Tarsus, as she should have been, 250
By savage Cleon. She shall tell thee all;
When thou shalt kneel and justify in knowledge
She is thy very princess. Who is this?
　　Hel. Sir, 'tis the Governor of Mytilene,
Who, hearing of your melancholy state, 255
Did come to see you.
　　Per.　　　　　　I embrace you.
Give me my robes. I am wild in my beholding.
O Heavens bless my girl! But, hark, what music?
Tell Helicanus, my Marina, tell him 260
O'er, point by point, for yet he seems to doubt,
How sure you are my daughter. But, what music?
　　Hel. My lord, I hear none.
　　Per. None!
The music of the spheres! List, my Marina. 265
　　Lys. It is not good to cross him. Give him way.
　　Per. Rarest sounds! Do ye not hear?
　　Lys. Music, my lord?
　　Per.　　　　　　I hear most heavenly music!
It nips me unto list'ning, and thick slumber 270
Hangs upon mine eyes. Let me rest.　　　*[Sleeps.]*
　　Lys. A pillow for his head.
So, leave him all. Well, my companion friends,
If this but answer to my just belief,
I'll well remember you.　　*[Exeunt all but Pericles.]* 275

Diana [appears to Pericles as in a vision].

282. **give them repetition to the life:** repeat them (the crosses) in exact detail.

283. **Or:** either.

284. **silver bow:** as goddess of the hunt, Diana was often portrayed with a bow, but this may refer to the bow of the crescent moon.

286. **argentine:** silver.

292. **blown:** swelling; **eftsoons:** soon.

Di. My temple stands in Ephesus. Hie thee thither
And do upon mine altar sacrifice.
There, when my maiden priests are met together,
Before the people all,
Reveal how thou at sea didst lose thy wife. 280
To mourn thy crosses, with thy daughter's, call,
And give them repetition to the life.
Or perform my bidding, or thou livest in woe;
Do it, and happy, by my silver bow!
Awake, and tell thy dream. [*Disappears.*] 285
   Per. Celestial Dian, goddess argentine,
I will obey thee. Helicanus!

[*Enter Helicanus, Lysimachus, and Marina.*]

   Hel. Sir?
   Per. My purpose was for Tarsus, there to strike
The inhospitable Cleon; but I am 290
For other service first. Toward Ephesus
Turn our blown sails: eftsoons I'll tell thee why.
[*To Lysimachus*] Shall we refresh us, sir, upon your
    shore,
And give you gold for such provision 295
As our intents will need?
   Lys. Sir,
With all my heart; and, when you come ashore,
I have another suit.
   Per. You shall prevail, 300
Were it to woo my daughter; for it seems
You have been noble toward her.

[V.ii.] Gower tells of the festivities in Mytilene in Pericles' honor. Marina and Lysimachus are betrothed but will not be married until Pericles has made his promised pilgrimage to Diana's temple at Ephesus.

⬛⬛⬛⬛⬛⬛⬛⬛⬛⬛⬛⬛⬛⬛⬛

5. **aptly:** readily; **suppose:** imagine.
12. **he:** i.e., Pericles.
14. **confound:** destroy.
15. **In feathered briefness:** with winged speed.
20. **your fancies' thankful doom:** i.e., your imaginations' decision, for which I must be thankful.

[Scene II.]

[Enter Gower, before the Temple of Diana at Ephesus.]

Now our sands are almost run;
More a little, and then dumb.
This, my last boon, give me,
For such kindness must relieve me,
That you aptly will suppose   5
What pageantry, what feats, what shows,
What minstrelsy and pretty din
The regent made in Mytilene,
To greet the King. So he thrived
That he is promised to be wived   10
To fair Marina; but in no wise
Till he had done his sacrifice,
As Dian bade: whereto being bound,
The interim, pray you, all confound.
In feathered briefness sails are filled,   15
And wishes fall out as they're willed.
At Ephesus the temple see,
Our king and all his company.
That he can hither come so soon
Is by your fancies' thankful doom.   20

                                        [Exit.]

escape

... at Mytilene. Thaisa, the high priestess, recognizes Pericles and faints. When she is revived and speaks, Pericles recognizes his wife and takes her in his arms. Marina is introduced to her long-lost mother and to Helicanus, and Thaisa presents Lord Cerimon, whose care revived her. Pericles proposes that Marina's marriage to Lysimachus be performed at Pentapolis. Hearing that Simonides is dead, he decides that Marina and Lysimachus shall reign in Tyre, while he and Thaisa rule Pentapolis.

7. **silver livery:** virginal white garb.
14. **favor:** appearance.
21. **Reverend appearer:** thou, who appear reverend (a polite address before contradicting him).